I WAS A STRANGER

A Pastor and Professor Quaker Mystery

# I Was a Stranger

by **Patricia Thomas**

**Friends United Press**

Friends United Press
101 Quaker Hill Drive
Richmond, IN 47374
info@fum.org
friendsunitedmeeting.org


Library of Congress Control Number: 2019953898
ISBN: 978-0-944350-84-3

Cover art by Rebecca Kinsinger Bowman

DEDICATION

For Doug, the real professor in my life

*N*o, not again! Only this time there were no gun shots, no screams of terror, yet the memory of his father's words urged him on. *Once you start to run, my son, do not stop. No matter what you hear behind you, remember Lot's wife, and never, never look back. For they come by night—the darkness is their friend. They will hunt you down, and when they catch you, my son, they will kill you. So— remember Lot's wife, and never, never look back.*

She caught a glimpse of him from her dormitory window, a thin, dark figure, slipping between the bushes lining the building's foundation walls. Movement inside the sweatshirt hood signaled his fright, and her body shivered in response. As he disappeared into the night, she thought she saw wisps of smoke curling up from the base of the building.

She strained her eyes, afraid of what she might be seeing; should she go out into the dark, where she had caught sight of the shadowy figure? As she waited, indecisive, she heard the sirens. Big, red fire trucks lumbered up the cul-de-sac. She shielded her eyes from the piercing lights and with a sigh, gently closed the heavy curtains.

# CHAPTER ONE

The week of the fire began innocuously enough. The still-warm October sun eased its way above the trees, erasing the thin layer of frost laid down the night before. Gray cement sidewalks crisscrossed the lush campus grass where sheep and cattle grazed in the years before Phineas Barrett donated his farm for an institution of higher education in 1871. A year later, Miss Hannah Elizabeth Emerick founded the Quaker School for Women, the only institution of its kind for hundreds of miles around.

Today, almost one hundred and fifty years later, Ruthalice Michels parked her two-door, lemon yellow Focus in its designated spot and gathered her belongings. She pulled open the solid oak door to Frame Meetinghouse, walked down the dimly lit corridor, and stopped in front of the Office of Campus Ministry.

Her fingers sorted through the crumpled tissue, gum wrappers, and assorted detritus at the bottom of her green canvas bag. "How is it possible to lose something that substantial?" she grumbled impatiently. "I know you're in there somewhere." She gave the bag another shake and dove back in. "Gotcha!" she exclaimed as her middle finger snagged the bulky key ring.

Flipping the keys over one at a time, she located number 74 and unlocked the office door. She hung her tweed cloak over the wobbly clothes tree, picked a slender, gray hair off the worsted fabric, then turned to stare at her reflection in the full-length mirror nailed to the back of the office door. A blue-eyed woman with straight-cut bangs and thick, French braid looked back at her. She placed a hand on each hip, sucked her tummy in, and executed two quarter turns, running an experienced eye down the practical, ankle-length, black cotton skirt.

"This is the day which our Lord has made, let us rejoice and be glad in it," she recited in her best preacher voice. "And," she added, her voice soft with gratitude, "thank you, most gracious God, for trusting me with another day." Ruthalice Michels, the fifty-one-year-old campus minister of Emerick College was ready for whatever the day might bring.

With a sigh of satisfaction, Ruthalice surveyed her headquarters. A scarred (though still serviceable) wooden desk occupied two-thirds of the south wall. Miscellaneous memorabilia picked up along life's journey were tucked between Bibles, volumes on spirituality, and an eclectic collection of resource books on the floor-to-ceiling shelves to her right. Orange squares of sticky paper covered with cryptic notes and to-do lists clung to the wall above the polished mahogany frame displaying her seminary diploma.

She crossed the room, seized the frayed pull cord, and raised the Venetian blinds. Sunlight glinted off the hand-painted sign of the Leaky Cup Coffee Café across Division Street, making it glow. Missy Springer, the café's proud proprietress attacked the wide, wooden porch with her broom, sending swirls of sand and dust particles down the front steps. Mother Nature and the local purveyor of rich, strong coffee had launched their day as well.

Settling into her desk chair, Ruthalice pulled the nearest Post-it note off the wall. "Looks like 'call Becky re lunch.'" Busy deciphering her own scrawl, she didn't hear the tentative knock on her door. The young woman tried a second time, striking the door twice with her knuckles, causing Ruthalice to jump.

"I didn't mean to startle you, Ruthalice."

"No problem," she replied, spinning her chair around. "Why, Rani Brown, how nice to see you again." She indicated the two overstuffed chairs on either side of a low coffee table. "Please have a seat."

The young woman took a quick look up and down the hallway, then closed the door behind her. Gathering her long, denim skirt around her legs, she chose the maroon and blue striped armchair. This left the flamboyant, orange alternative for the campus minister. Painfully aware that her extra-large white blouse, strewn with scarlet-red cherries, clashed horribly with the chair's unfortunate color, Ruthalice sat down anyway and reached under the coffee table for the lighter, taking in the young woman across from her as she lit the fat candle on the table between them.

Rani seemed more nervous than usual. In fact, Rani seemed intently focused on a cluster of colorful little dolls in her right hand.

"Those are worry dolls, aren't they?" Ruthalice said. She slid the box of tissue that lived on the table within easy reach, in case the young woman burst into tears.

"Is everything all right at home? I think the last time we talked, your father was looking for a job. I'm sure that's just as difficult in Jamaica, if not more so, than in the United States."

Rani nodded. "They had just moved to Kingston. Now Papa manages The Big Blue Mountain Coffee Shoppe down by the harbor on Port Royal Street in Kingston." Her eyes shone brightly with pride.

"I love Blue Mountain Coffee," Ruthalice exclaimed. "Wouldn't it be great if we could talk the Leaky Cup into serving it as one of their specialty coffees?"

Rani shrugged and pulled a pink tissue from the box. Ruthalice crossed her legs at the ankle and leaned back into her chair while Rani dabbed her eyes. With fifteen years of pastoral care ministry under her belt, Ruthalice Michels understood that every person who passed through her door carried the possibility of exposing the dark side of human nature and knocking the day's best laid plans to smithereens in the process.

"I heard two students in the bathroom," Rani began softly. "I didn't mean to listen, but they were talking so loudly I could hear them over the running water."

Ruthalice counted to twenty, then fifty. "Rani," she nudged finally, "What were they talking about?"

"A fire." Her fingers picked at the doll's embroidered face.

"What sort of fire?"

Rani shrugged. "'It's going to be so awesome, we'll be the talk of the town,'" she quoted.

Ruthalice began to push the soft wax into the candle flame with her right index finger. "I'm a firm believer in woman's intuition, Rani, so what's your sense of what's going on here?"

Rani squeezed her jaw shut as if to trap any words of speculation that might inadvertently slip out.

"Have you told your resident advisor?"

"Yes."

"And?"

"She thinks they're talking about the homecoming bonfire."

"That doesn't make sense. Homecoming was last Friday." Ruthalice stretched her legs, taking a moment to admire the shiny toes of her new black boots. Rani's attention slipped back to her little bundle. The dolls' faces looked in danger of being rubbed raw.

"Yes." She hesitated. "The louder girl said she had collected all the necessary ingredients."

A door opened at the end of the hallway. The sound of student voices returning cell phone calls signaled the end of class. Rani got to her feet and slung her backpack over her left shoulder. Ruthalice reached out and lightly touched her arm.

"I know it was difficult for you, Rani, but I'm grateful you shared your concern with me."

"The loud girl is Priscilla Brinkley."

Rani opened the door and stepped into the hallway, becoming just another student exiting Frame Meetinghouse.

# CHAPTER TWO

After lunch at the Leaky Cup Coffee Café, Ruthalice ambled across campus to Jones Student Center. After collecting her mail, she reported the morning's conversation with Rani Brown to Barbara "Babs" Carroll, the dean of students, who assured her the housing staff would keep their ears open for rumors about any talk of fire.

Back outside, Ruthalice walked across campus to Fox Administration where she hoped to have a chat with Mary Scott, secretary to the academic dean. Mary possessed an uncanny ability to discern when a confidential bit of information passed along might help the campus minister go about the business of providing pastoral care to the college community. *Where in the world would campus ministers like me be without allies like you, dear Mary?*

Ruthalice pulled open the heavy glass door and immediately spotted Theodore Cope slumped on the bench outside the academic dean's office. His right hand was encased in a brand-new and as-yet-unautographed white plaster cast.

*My goodness, don't you look as though you'd rather be any place but here,* she thought, remembering Coach Bob Stevens's recent comment that his starting goalkeeper had an attitude problem. Ted stared at the floor between his feet, his elbows resting on his thighs.

"Hey, Ted," she said lightly. "Mind if I sit down?"

A disinterested shrug was his only acknowledgement. Undeterred by the obvious lack of enthusiasm,

Ruthalice settled herself on the bench, aware of the light touch of their hips. The young man shifted away, putting a fraction of an inch between them.

"Saw your shutout Saturday night. That was a heck of a win for the Mighty Quakers."

"Yeah."

"So, what's up with the cast?"

Theodore Cope, the most highly recruited goalie in the forty-year history of the Mighty Quakers men's soccer program, leaned on his left elbow, taking the weight off his right arm. Ruthalice pictured the conclusion of Saturday's soccer match: ecstatic Emerick players leaping into a heap of bodies on top of the goalie. Even though her husband, Cliff—as an ex-football player—adamantly maintained that these victory pileups were a normal form of healthy, male bonding, Ruthalice remained convinced this victory ritual was a disaster waiting to happen.

"Bit of bad luck, that," she said, watching the side of his face, "So what happened?"

Ted slumped, his legs extended straight out in front of him and glared at the wall. Wary of coming off as overbearingly parental, Ruthalice waited him out.

"The Red Knights are a friggin' bunch of damn sore losers." He rubbed his cast with his left hand. "There weren't nothing cheap about my shutout. How's it my fault the ref called an obvious hand ball on the Knights' midfielder?"

*Thus, nullifying the goal that would have tied the game up.*

"It was a pretty controversial call, though, which fortunately went our way. And that?" she asked, nodding at his right hand. Ruthalice watched the EC star goalie wrestle with just how much confession was good for his soul.

"I slammed the gym locker and broke my hand." Ted's knuckles turned white as he clenched the bench with his left hand. "Now I'm out for the rest of the season. It sucks!"

"It sucks all right," Ruthalice commented dryly, adopting the I'm-with-you-on-this-one approach. Ted favored her with an amused half-smile. "I broke my right arm five months before my wedding. Had to bribe a girlfriend to address all our invitations for me. It was a real nuisance."

Ted raised his eyebrows slightly as if to say, "Yeah, so?"

"You right-handed, too?"

He gave a sullen nod.

Ruthalice shifted gears. "Are you in academic difficulty?" Praying she wasn't about to overstep her bounds, she added, "If not, surely Coach Stevens will let you sit on the bench with the team."

"Look, the only reason I'm at EC is to play soccer." His voice grew surly. "My father said, 'You don't play soccer, Me and mom aren't wasting our money on college.'" Ted banged his head back against the wall with a thud. "The old man's quick to remind me it's my mother's half-baked fancy that her firstborn needs a college education in order to amount to something. 'I don't have no GED and I've done just fine, thank you very much. And I don't owe anybody nothing.'"

"So, your parents are coming to get you?"

"Not yet." Ted shifted uncomfortably. "Student insurance paid for the cast and trip to the Boone County Hospital, so I haven't called them yet." Ted's eyes hardened. "I'm dropping out and beating dad to the punch."

The office door swung open.

"Dean Feller will see you now, Theodore."

Mary Scott waited while he hoisted his backpack onto his left shoulder then followed him into the outer office. As Ruthalice bent to collect the mail, which had slipped off the bench and scattered underneath it, Mary stepped through the doorway and strode briskly down the corridor. Finished straightening the pile and firmly tucking it against her chest, Ruthalice stepped out into the hall, looking for Mary, but she had already disappeared. Ruthalice shrugged, decided to try again at a more opportune time, and headed back to Frame.

Back in her own office, Ruthalice settled into the striped chair, closed her eyes, and waited for the internal voice to stop chattering, but like the voice of St. Luke's persistent widow before the hard-hearted judge, Rani Brown's fears continued to pester her. Realizing her only defense was to get up and act, Ruthalice walked to her desk, turned on the computer, and pulled up the student directory.

Barton, Beasley—she ran her index finger down the screen. Bosner, Bradley, Brinkley. "Ah, Brinkley, Priscilla—D104. Well, Ms. Brinkley, I'll just pop by and see if I get lucky, and if not, at least I will have done something."

As she let herself in to Douglas Hall, Bruce Springsteen's voice, unhampered by six-inch cinder block walls, sang her down the hallway to Room 104.

"Someone's home," she surmised wryly, pounding on the door with her fist. She was about to try again when Bruce was cut off mid-chorus and the door swung open.

"What." The disembodied word lay somewhere between a bored question and a disinterested statement.

"I'd like to talk with you, Priscilla. May I come in?"

The young woman shrugged, moved out of the way,

and dropped down in the middle of a beautifully made bed. Stepping through the doorway Ruthalice felt as though she'd just fallen down the rabbit hole and landed smack dab on the cover of *Better Homes and Gardens!* Pale green draperies secured with gold-tasseled tiebacks hung gracefully on either side of the metal-framed window. Bedspreads, pillows, and throw rugs in bright, contemporary colors and patterns complemented the light blue, cinder block walls. Two, framed posters of castles somewhere in the mountains of Europe hung over a family-heirloom, mahogany desk. Except for a ratty, brown terrycloth bathrobe in the middle of the second bed, this dormitory room was ready for inspection by the fussiest boarding school matron.

Ruthalice was impressed. *Suzy done told me when it comes to interior decorating, nothing beats good taste and a whole lot of money!*

"Priscilla, I had no idea a college room could look this good. You've created a veritable oasis in here!"

"My mother is a frustrated interior decorator." It sounded like a curse, the suffering daughter's cross to bear. "She takes it out on my rooms."

Ignoring the resentment radiating from the blue-blooded young woman lounging on the bed, Ruthalice got to the point.

"I understand you're planning a spectacular fire."

Priscilla blinked: "A fire."

"Someone's concerned enough to report a conversation she overheard in the bathroom."

Priscilla frowned. "Oh yeah, now I remember. Some of us were bragging on how awesome the homecoming bonfire was going to be." Ruthalice followed her gaze to the framed photo of herself in an Emerick cheerleader outfit holding a pompom in each hand, arms stretched high over her head. "I'm captain of the spirit squad," Priscilla added, sounding as though that explained everything.

"But this conversation occurred last night, after homecoming," Ruthalice stated. "Tell me about it."

"Your little eavesdropper has been busy. What's she trying to prove?"

"You said, 'I've all the ingredients I need. It's going to be so awesome, we'll be the talk of the town,' or words to that effect."

Priscilla's stare hardened. "If you must know, we were talking about decorations for a twenty-first birthday party for one of the girls in the house." Priscilla crossed her arms. "That's allowed on this campus, isn't it?"

"Who's the lucky girl?"

"Regina Faulkner."

"Regina's in my Bible class. I'll be sure to wish her the best." Turning to go, Ruthalice placed her hand on the doorknob, then turned back to say, "Thanks for clearing this up for me, Priscilla. Is it a surprise party?"

"Not really." Priscilla picked up her cell phone. "Are we done?"

"I believe so," Ruthalice replied, "at least for the time being."

# CHAPTER THREE

Thirty-five minutes later, Ruthalice bounced up the tree-lined lane of Horsefeathers Farm in her lemon-yellow, two-door Focus. A large UPS box leaned against the front door.

"Cool, our new blanket's here." Ruthalice closed the garage door, walked around the side of the house, and climbed the porch steps. She inhaled the sweet smell of ripe corn and let out a contented sigh. On this very spot eleven months ago, Clifford P. Mowry had bowed from the waist and escorted her across the threshold.

"Welcome to Horsefeathers, the Mowry Centennial Farm, Ruthalice Michels," he had said, beaming from ear to ear. "It's our home now."

"You know what I'm thinking?" she had asked, as she wrapped both arms around his neck. "You and I wouldn't be standing here today as husband and wife if Drew hadn't suffered that heart attack and Julia hadn't gotten fed up 30 years ago with playing second fiddle to your passion for hunting mollusks twenty-four seven. There would be no Michels and Mowry, no minister and malacologist."

"No M&Ms," they had intoned as one.

"I had no idea what the future held when I set out for a whole new life, moving to Colorado to join the Park Service."

"And then coming back home when Emerick College was looking for a tenure-track biology professor."

Cliff had nodded and added, "Now, don't forget the best part." Ruthalice had raised an inquisitive eyebrow.

"I'd lived in that campus condo for nearly sixteen years, when one extraordinary day the new campus minister moved in next door. And the rest," he had continued, gently wrapping a stray strand of brown hair behind her left ear, "as they say, is history."

*Whew*, she thought, propping the screen door open with one foot, *this whole how-we-got-together thing still gives me goosebumps.*

Ruthalice stepped into the living room, set the blanket box on the floor and headed down the Walkway of the Ancestors, her name for the formidable gallery of oil paintings, beginning with Cliff's great-great-great grandfather Mowry, which lined the corridor from the front room to the kitchen. The kitchen, whose single nod to the 21st century had been a Lowe's floor model, high-efficiency refrigerator and a microwave left over from Cliff's years of bachelorhood, had been Ruthalice's first project. Her addition of a breakfast nook with red vinyl-covered facing benches and Tiffany chandelier had quickly become a favored location for mutual checking in at the start and finish of each day.

Ruthalice dumped her canvas bag on the counter and rummaged through the pantry cupboard. Twenty-five minutes later a truck door slammed, and Cliff materialized in the mudroom. He kicked off his hand-tooled Western boots and stepped sock-footed into the kitchen.

"What's for supper?" he asked, giving both Ruthalice and the chili-covered wooden spoon in her hand an enormous hug. He dropped his keys into the basket on the windowsill and inhaled. "Can't eat chili without crackers," he said, yanking the snack drawer open. He winced as Ruthalice plopped a large spoonful of rice into her bowl and buried it under chili. Though a bona fide malacologist with a PhD from The Ohio State University, Clifford P. Mowry remained a farm boy from the top of his curly, red hair to the bottoms of his size twelve feet. Rice, though a passable side dish if dowsed with enough soy sauce, did not belong under chili.

The newlyweds clasped hands across the table and offered a silent blessing. Five minutes later Cliff led off their nightly ritual of catching up on each other's day.

"So, what fires did the campus minister extinguish today?"

Ruthalice grabbed the plaid napkin off her lap as a coughing fit seized her.

"Oh dear, excuse me." She shook her head and dabbed at her watering eyes. "It's just that you couldn't have picked a more apt metaphor."

Cliff looked puzzled.

"You asked about extinguishing fires."

Cliff dumped another handful of crackers on the chili residue in the bottom of the bowl and picked up his spoon. "Go on."

"Rani Brown came to my office this morning distressed about a conversation she overheard in the women's bathroom between Priscilla Brinkley and another student. They were talking about an awesome fire—quote, unquote. I touched all the bases I could today; Babs has her residence hall advisors on alert for any rumors. I paid a visit to Priscilla, who is innocent as the day is long." She emptied her glass of milk, then rubbed any tomato sauce or milk mustache off her upper lip. "So, we'll just have to wait and see if anything comes of it."

She leaned back against the padded cushion. "A few students dribbled in with various excuses for missing the scheduled Bible test. I kept reminding myself I'm not their mother, let alone some Universal Voice of Conscience."

Cliff chuckled sympathetically.

"A parent called asking why we allow anti-war pro-testors to hold signs and pass out literature on campus, so I patiently explained our Quaker Peace Testimony, that we strive to live a life which 'takes away the occasion of all war' and the importance of publicly stating these principles as clearly as possible."

"And did you agree to politely disagree?"

"He didn't slam the phone down when he hung up on me."

Ruthalice slipped the two-inch gold hoop out of her left ear and massaged the lobe with her thumb and middle finger.

"And you, dear heart? What transpired in the hallowed halls of Dalton Science Building?"

"A friend of yours showed up expecting me to solve her enormous problem!"

"Oh no, not again."

"Yup, your old childhood buddy, Mrs. H. She came to inform me she's been inundated with disgusting things—that's her term not mine by the way—and proceeded to pontificate on how these creatures are consuming her mums at an alarming rate. She used a painful number of scientifically vague and therefore useless terminology." He sighed. "I finally agreed to look at a sample if she would bring one into my office."

Ruthalice crossed her arms: "Your first mistake."

"Apparently. She shrieked, 'There's no way on God's green earth I'm touching one of those slimy, nasty things. You're the scientist here, not me; you know how to handle all sorts of objectionable creatures.'"

Cliff rolled his eyes.

"There's more?"

"There's more. 'You only teach two classes and a lab so surely you can find a half hour sometime today to conduct a proper investigation.'"

Ruthalice burst out laughing. "I've told you that when Suzanne Matilda Polk Henson has an emergency, it's a crisis of biblical proportion."

Cliff fiddled with his spoon, turning it over and over between his thumb and forefinger.

"Quickly ascertaining there'd be no peace in heaven or on earth until I relented, I proceeded directly to Henson's Formal Gardens, collection jar in hand."

"So, pray tell, what IS this dreadful creature busily consuming Suzy's mums?"

"Actually, it's the not so common *Limax maximus!*"

"*Limax* whoimus?"

"The leopard slug, a rather impressive little critter. *Limax maximus* are wrinkled and grayish-yellow with four tentacles. Usually nocturnal, they will sometimes come out when it rains. Oh, and they leave a lovely, long cushion of mucus slime."

"I love it!" Ruthalice clapped her hands and rested them on her stomach. "Dear Suzy, the best next-door neighbor a lost little girl could wish for. You know, Cliff, after Natalie OD'd in the upstairs bathroom, and my father's reasons for absenteeism came to sound more and more disingenuous, Suzy essentially moved in. She became my surrogate mom, or as she liked to say, 'Mommy Numero Duo.'"

"Natalie being your biological and therefore Mommy Numero Uno."

"In name only," Ruthalice added quietly. Then she smiled. "Well, Mommy Numero Duo, you sure picked the right man for the job."

"You know my motto: 'Malacologists to the Rescue.'"

"Let's see if I can remember." Ruthalice tilted her head back and gazed at the ceiling as if the definition were written beside the Tiffany chandelier. "Malacology, the branch of zoology dealing with mollusks, the second largest phylum of animals in terms of described species."

"Give that woman an A." Cliff placed both elbows on the table and pointed an imaginary piece of chalk in her direction. "Now tell me young lady, how many existing species of mollusks have been identified?"

"One hundred thousand," she said, sitting up straight and returning his mischievous grin. "Furthermore, because Ohio boasts an unusual number of species of freshwater clams, The Nature Conservancy has designated our fair state, quote, a hot spot for clam biodiversity, unquote."

"Well done, my dear, well done!"

Cliff stretched his legs under the table and rested his knee against her leg. Ruthalice picked at a blob of red wax stuck in the weave of her placemat.

"Actually, I confess I never heard of a leopard slug." She rested her head against the high cushioned back of the breakfast nook bench. "I assume it has spots."

"Indeed. Four inches in length, loves mushrooms, even eats the occasional slug." Cliff gave a pensive sigh. "In the interest of academic honesty, I was forced to admit it's highly unlikely the leopard slug is her culprit. However, I did suggest that by importing toads and turtles she could reduce the number of *Limax maximus* in her garden, but Ms. H. gave me the distinct impression my findings as well as my latest helpful hint left something to be desired." He smiled ruefully. "But that's often the way of scientific inquiry."

Ruthalice lifted the forest green shawl she'd left on the bench at breakfast and pulled it over her shoulders.

"Moses didn't really part the Red Sea, you know."

"Really. How so?"

"After our quiz this morning, a kid produced an article from the *LA Times* explaining the entire episode as a natural event using wind speed, the moon's gravitational pull, and the depth of the water." She shook her head and smiled. "I wonder sometimes at our human need to explain everything scientifically. I'm content with the occasional miracle now and again."

They cleared the table and moved to the living room as darkness slowly closed the view of the meadow behind the house. Finding nothing of interest in the *Boone County Bugle*, Ruthalice folded the newspaper and waited until Cliff looked up from his book.

"Do you have Ted Cope in class?"

"Not this semester. He's the soccer goalie who broke his wrist after that game we saw Saturday. Word has it he's dropping out of school."

Cliff slipped the torn envelope he was using as a bookmark between the pages and laid *The Rustlers of Pecos County*, first edition Zane Grey, on the end table. Seeing Ruthalice's scowl, he added, "Am I to deduce you're involved in this somehow?"

"It's his hand actually." She removed her glasses and rubbed the bridge of her nose. "Apparently, Papa's going to be royally fried."

"Is 'fried' a theological term?" Cliff grinned and squeezed her hand.

"Ted said going to college is his mother's idea and made it pretty clear that as soon as his dad finds out, he'll insist Ted gets his fanny back to the farm and stop wasting his time and money in college. I don't know how much help he'll be this fall. He's not going to be able to lift anything."

"He can still run the combine."

She conceded the point with a shrug and put her wire-rimmed glasses back on her nose. "I've never met Ted's dad, but I hear Oakes Quarry's finest have escorted his mercurial uncle from many a Little League game for yelling obscenities at the refs." Ruthalice slipped her thick silver-flecked braid over her shoulder and began brushing its soft, fluffy tip along her cheek.

"Just remember, honey, Ted's dad Roger has lived his entire life as Sidney Cope's kid brother. Sid Cope made a killing selling off the frontage after inheriting his half of the farm from their dad. There's no question Sidney Cope thinks rather highly of himself. Most folks around here, however, know him as an impetuous but shrewd wheeler-dealer."

Cliff stifled a yawn and stood up.

"I don't know a soul in Boone County who doesn't have great sympathy for Roger Cope, but I do feel badly for that son of his." He grasped Ruthalice's hands and pulled her up. "Theodore's bright enough to make it in college and with some encouragement will certainly make a comfortable living even if he doesn't want to farm. I suspect his Uncle Sidney is the proverbial bull in the china shop who will throw his weight around whenever it works to his advantage. How Sid Cope will view his one and only nephew's withdrawal is anybody's guess."

The M&Ms headed down the hallway turning off lights as they went. Ten minutes later Ruthalice lay in bed listening to Cliff's gentle snoring. *Ted...Priscilla...*

*Ted...Priscilla* his breathing seemed to say. Rolling over on her left side, Ruthalice draped an arm over Cliff's chest. Up and down, in and out. *Ted...Priscilla. What was it about those two? The hot-headed farm boy and the bored little rich girl each angry and alone, fighting personal demons in their own problematic way.*

She stared out the east-facing window at the rising moon.

"Dear God, I surrender the world and all the hurting people to your loving care. And please," she added closing her eyes, "don't let there be a latent arsonist in our midst, OK? Amen."

## CHAPTER FOUR

"Oh, what a beautiful morning, oh, what a beautiful day!" Ruthalice sang lustily as she gazed through the thick, wavy window glass above the kitchen sink. The hackberry trees rippled gently as though under water. A cardinal-red blur flitted into a cedar on the edge of the yard as the early sun edged the west pasture in fresh morning light.

"I'm one incredibly lucky girl," she informed the spider industriously constructing her silky house in the corner of the window frame. "Eleven months, four days and some hours ago, I promised for the second time to be a 'loving and faithful wife for as long as we both shall live.'"

Ruthalice gave herself an enormous bear hug and sashayed across the living room to the rear of the house, straightening pillows and magazines as she went. "Not only did I manage to procure the proverbial cake, I'm happily devouring it too. How cool is that?"

Ruthalice flipped on the overhead light and wandered into the enormous walk-in closet. "It's your wedding present," Cliff's mother informed him as she announced her plan to knock out the south wall of the master bedroom. "Your father and I are remodeling the old hired-hand cottage," Mary Esther announced the moment she and Samuel learned of their son's intention to marry the campus minister. "We've lived in this house for fifty-five years. Now it's your turn."

Ruthalice made her selection from the impressive collection of oversized shirts and tugged her black skirt over her head. She slipped a pair of gold hoops through her ears, added five matching bracelets of varying widths and, voila! *Lose twenty-five pounds and you're one elegant woman!*

"Easier said than done," she reminded herself as she gathered up her purse and jacket, heading out to her car. "You've conveniently forgotten our predilection for all things chocolate!" Ruthalice backed out of the garage and coasted down the gravel driveway. Clumps of Queen Anne's lace, chicory, goldenrod, and ironweed dotted the hillside. creating clusters of white, pale blue, gold, and purple.

Twenty minutes later she pulled into the spot reserved for the campus minister, shut the car door, and headed for her office. She loved the click-click sound of her boots on the well-worn, wooden floor of Frame Meetinghouse. She loved the fact that each of the eight-foot solid oak interior doors had a glass transom at the top, a leftover from pre-air conditioning days. A small library, two bathrooms, and a seminar room ran the length of the corridor between the parking lot and the spacious room at the south end of the building where Oakes Quarry Friends held meeting for worship every First Day morning. Across the hall, the Office of Campus Ministry was lodged between the old coat closet—now housing the janitorial supplies—and Room 6, the larger of the two classrooms.

Ruthalice unlocked her office door and wandered to her desk, gently touching the face of Professor Clifford Mowry smiling at her from a green bamboo frame. Resplendent in brown rubber wading boots, his khaki, broad-brimmed hat cocked at a rakish angle, her hubby stood hip deep in the waters of the Little Miami River. She waited until the icons finished appearing on her computer screen, typed a short love note, and hit Send.

"I hope your day's off to a great start, my darling Clifford."

Two hours earlier Professor Clifford P. Mowry shoved a copy of *Science* magazine into the outer pocket of his briefcase and alighted from his black Dodge Ram. In his L.L. Bean denim jeans, deep loden-green, v-neck sweater and pinstriped, button-down shirt, Cliff looked every bit the rugged park service ranger. His lanky, 6'2" frame easily carried the twenty pounds gained since graduate school and government service.

Cliff deftly skirted a sodden pile of brown leaves clogging the storm drain and strode the short distance to the science building. From the moment he'd set foot on campus as the new professor of biology, Cliff had admired the exquisite workmanship of Dalton Hall. Massive beige foundation blocks supported the stately brick building, each stone dug, cut, and hauled by teams of horses from the Old Oakes Quarry three miles southwest of town. Heavy, leaded windows and a green copper roof added to Dalton's strength of character. Named in honor of the mid-19th-century British Quaker chemist John Dalton, the hall was built in 1882, the third and last of the original buildings. President Wilbur Starbuck referred to the Three Sisters in his commencement speech to the class of 1902, and the name stuck. Penington Place, Fox Hall, and Dalton Science Hall form a loosely drawn L, denoting the perimeter of the original Quaker School for Women.

Cliff bounded up the stairs and walked down the hall into his office. He threw his jacket over the back of his office chair, grabbed his magazine off the desk, donned a stained white lab coat as he headed out into the hallway, and entered the classroom across the hall.

After he distributed biology exams to the students perched on lab stools around the table, he spent the next hour proctoring the midterm, answering the occasional question, and devouring an article on "The Habitat Requirements for the Host Fish of Freshwater Mussels."

At precisely 8:55 a.m., Charles "Curly" Hopkins slid an overstuffed accordion file under his right arm and left his office on the second floor of Fox Hall. Using the sleeve of his left arm, he polished the bronze plaque affixed to the door—Charles E. Hopkins, Professor of History—and muttered under his breath, "I've been the sole professor in EC's History Department for sixty-odd years and all I've got to show for it is a plaque with my name on it." Though he never complained to the half-dozen students in his senior seminar, the professor's colleagues had heard it all before. "I will show this college the sturdy stuff of which Charles Evelyn Hopkins is forged, as it is my intention to lecture until my voice gives out or my brain atrophies, whichever body part betrays me first."

At the bottom of the stairs, he hit the exit bar and stepped outside, inhaled a deep satisfying lungful of crisp October air, and headed for DH201 on the second floor of Dalton Science Hall. He let himself in, sat down in the wobbly visitor's chair, and began drumming his fingers on the side of his accordion file until the rightful occupant stepped through the doorway.

Passing his not unexpected guest, Cliff dropped twenty-three bluebooks on his desk and smiled fondly at the college curmudgeon. "Charles is an avid researcher with a healthy dose of skepticism for secondary sources," Cliff explained to Ruthalice during dinner one night after grumbling about the amount of time

Charles had taken out of his already busy day. "He spends the weekends sequestered in the same library carrel assigned to him when he joined the faculty in the mid-seventies. I'm willing to be his sounding board because I discovered years ago that under all that crustiness there beats a several-times-broken, but nonetheless compassionate heart."

"So," Cliff began as he crossed his arms and leaned back in his chair. "Who is this week's worthy addition to the manuscript?"

"Bishop Swithun, humble advocate for the poor and sick whose shrine drew thousands of pilgrims not only from all over England, but the continent as well. According to tradition, if it rains on Saint Swithun's bridge in Winchester on July 15th, the good saint's feast day, it will continue to rain for forty days." Cliff smiled as Charles added that piece of extraneous trivia.

"Travelers between Winchester and Canterbury Cathedrals established what would eventually be known as the Pilgrim's Way, made famous in literature, of course, by Geoffrey Chaucer's *Canterbury Tales*."

Charles shook his head and gazed out the window. "My schoolmates and I couldn't wait to reach the naughty bits we'd heard so much about, so we slogged through Chaucer's tortured Middle English with its quaint spelling and cumbersome poetic lines with adolescent anticipation."

Reminiscences of boyhoods in the heartlands of England and Ohio continued until the yellow warbler on the Audubon bird clock above Cliff's office door chirped a cheery ten o'clock *tsee-tsee-tsee* song, signaling the end of today's session. Charles rocked his 260-pound frame up and out of the visitor's chair and winked mischievously. "Clifford, my friend, there's more to this tale than meets the eye, and I plan to reveal all the twists and turns in my fifth book, *The Political Impact of Religious Pilgrims on the British Isles*." With a hearty "Cheerio!" Charles wandered back to Fox Hall, taking with him Cliff's last excuse to avoid grading the stack of newly minted exams.

# CHAPTER FIVE

I t was almost four before Ruthalice found time to go searching for Coach Bob Stevens. She followed the shouts and clapping of fall practice sessions to the athletics compound. Stevens stood at mid field, his whistle clenched between his teeth, watching the players execute their passing drills. Ruthalice leaned against the chain link fence, content to watch the choreographed dance of bodies and legs accompanied by the thump of feet striking leather balls. Coach Stevens turned the players loose for a scrimmage game and headed to the sidelines.

"Hey, Ruthalice, looking for me?" She nodded as he joined her at the edge of the playing field.

"I had a disconcerting exchange with your keeper yesterday, Bob. He told me he's dropping out of school."

"What exactly did Theodore say?" The coach leaned his right hip against the fence and crossed his arms.

"That the only reason his dad let him come to Emerick College in the first place was so he could play soccer, and now that he can't finish the season, Ted's decided to beat his father to the punch and withdraw." Ruthalice searched Bob's face. "Why am I getting the feeling there's more to this story?"

Coach Stevens removed his EC ball cap and scratched his head, letting his blond hair fall forward across his forehead. He replaced his hat, then began to smooth out some visible-only-to-him lumps in the playing field with his right foot. Apparently satisfied, he raised his head.

"I put Ted on probation for his conduct after Saturday's game."

"For slamming his locker and breaking his hand?!" Ruthalice realized that sounded like an accusation of overkill, but Bob cut in before she could backtrack and apologize.

"Is that what he told you?" Coach Stevens scowled at something over her left shoulder. "Let me put the record straight. Cope and four of his teammates went to Slippery Sue's after the game to celebrate the shutout and met up with two Red Knights who just happened to be there at the same time. The guys got into a shoving match after which the club's bouncer tossed them all out and called the cops." He flattened more lumps in the grass. "By the time the police arrived, the two Knights had bloody faces and Ted Cope had broken his right hand. So, yours truly spent most of what remained of Saturday night in the hospital waiting room so I could escort Theodore Cope back to Gurney Residence Hall." Bob shoved his hands deep into the pockets of his sweatpants. "I'm not happy about any of this, Ruthalice," he said sounding annoyed. "The truth is I was planning to keep the entire incident in-house. You can see how well that plan is working."

They shared the weary smile of veterans who'd weathered many a student's emotional outburst.

"So, Ted can't play anymore this fall because one, he's broken his hand, and two, he's on disciplinary probation for the fight." Coach Stevens nodded. "Do you suppose he's withdrawing from EC merely to prevent his father from having the satisfaction of winning this round?"

"Ted flies by the seat of his pants. He makes rash decisions, which is why he's one of the best goal keepers I've had in fifteen years of coaching." Stevens studied Ruthalice's face and sighed. "He's consumed with anger right now: at me, at his dad, at the college, probably at God, too, while he's at it." He smiled.

"Might he try to even the score?"

Stevens shrugged. "Ted's a hothead, so it's possible, but somehow I doubt it." Bob fiddled with his whistle, sliding it back and forth along the neck chain. "I checked with Dean Feller this morning. She's encouraged Ted to give himself the rest of the week before making a final decision. If on Monday he's still determined to drop out of school, she will fill out the paperwork to make it official."

"Have you heard from his father?"

"Roger?" He shook his head. "Not yet." Stevens moved a step closer. "To tell you the truth, Ruthalice, I'm way more concerned about Ted's uncle, Sidney Cope. You talk about short fuses and china-shop behavior." Bob shook his head, then grinned and pointed at the sky. "Put in a word with the Big Guy for me, will ya, Pastor Michels? I welcome help from all quarters."

"I'll see what I can do," Ruthalice replied, grinning. "In the meantime, Bob, holler if you think of anything more I should know." She turned to go, then turned back to ask, "Ted's still on campus?'

"He was as of this noon." Bob blew his whistle and the team sprinted over to collect their athletic bags. As the players trotted back to the locker room, their cleats clattered on the asphalt pathway. Ruthalice wandered the length of the field, letting her fingers bounce lightly over the chain links, then made a right-hand turn behind the goal posts. She paused at the parking lot on the north side of the field as a silver Mercedes-Benz GLC 300 rolled to a stop.

"Hey, Stevens," the driver yelled through the open window. "You and I need to talk." Sidney Cope slammed the car door and trudged angrily across the soccer field, his black trench coat flapping around him. Ruthalice watched as he positioned himself squarely in front of the coach.

"He really is every bit the schoolyard bully," Ruthalice said. She took a long, deep breath. "God, it would be really good if you would protect Bob Stevens right now; put him in one of those enormous plastic bubbles so he doesn't get punched out. Grant him tons of courage and boatloads of patience." She paused. "And may both these men find words to express their disappointment and love for young Theodore."

# CHAPTER SIX

The impossibly loud chimes jarred her awake. Ruthalice groped for her cell phone on the bedside table and peered at the bright green numerals on the digital clock. *Two-thirty. This cannot be good news.* She cleared her throat of nighttime phlegm.

"Ruthalice here."

"Mary Scott," came the brisk reply. "Penington Place is burning. The OQ fire department has just arrived on the scene."

Now fully awake, Ruthalice swung her legs over the edge of the bed. "Is anybody hurt?"

"We're getting a few complaints about the smoke, but since no one is in Penn Place at night..." Her voice faltered. "President Willson wants all staff and senior administrators on campus to help maintain order, which is why," she hastily explained, "I'm calling the campus minister in the middle of the night." Mary sighed. "It's all pretty chaotic right now, Ruthalice."

"I'll be at the meetinghouse as fast as I can, Mary."

Cliff raised his head. "Now what?" He reconsidered. "Off to campus?" Even in his groggy state of mind that seemed obvious. "Who was it?"

Ruthalice fell back across the bed, took his face in both hands and kissed him firmly on the forehead. "Answered in the order asked: Penington Place is on fire, yes, and Mary Scott."

"Sounds like all hands on deck," Cliff mumbled into his pillow.

"Nope, not yet, just the administrative staff, which means that you, my dear, lowly, tenured biology professor, can go back to sleep."

Ruthalice rolled back across the bed, heaved herself up, and headed to the closet to grab a navy-blue skirt and a pair of wool socks. "Yikes, it's already two-forty-five." She braided her hair and dashed across the living room, tugging the EC sweatshirt over her head. She nuked a mug of last night's cold coffee and slammed the mudroom door behind her. Seconds later, still wrestling with the seat belt, the campus minister raced down the driveway, spraying pellets of gravel into the grass.

Cliff tossed and turned until the down-filled quilt slid off the bed. "Something doesn't fit here," he said. He headed for the shower turning the faucet handle to "H." The scalding hot water pelted his back and ran down his legs. "The Building and Grounds Committee authorized a complete remodel of Penn Place including a total rewire."

Cliff toweled off, his thoughts still on the six-month process. Every time they met, Charles had shared his little joke: "Penington Place is the oldest building on campus by nine years. Charles Evelyn Hopkins is the oldest professor on campus by nine years. But by Jove, I'm less expensive to maintain!" The first few times the BGC members chuckled appreciatively, but over time, per usual, the joke wore thin. By the end of the semester they tended to ignore him.

"Sad," Cliff reflected, wondering which he meant, the man or the fire, "All those college historical records and one-of-a-kind Quaker books in the second floor reading room. My God, the old historian will go ballistic."

He dug his keys out of the pocket of his corduroy jacket and backed the truck out of the garage. As he drove into Oakes Quarry, the thick, black finger of smoke expanded and rose relentlessly into the star-studded sky. The entire scene was backlit by the neon street lights of town. He finally located a parking spot two blocks from campus. "Ruthalice's here somewhere," he muttered as he worked his way through the maze of emergency vehicles. He stopped in front of Dalton Hall and surveyed the campus green.

Penington Place was the center of attention, the other buildings mere kids gathered around the edges at a campfire. The sharp rotating lights of fire trucks and police vehicles penetrated the darkness. Hoses like enormous yellow snakes wound through the grass. An occasional shout from a fireman added to the drama. Despite the frenzy of activity, an ominous sense of foreboding was beginning to settle on the campus.

A half-hour earlier Ruthalice felt it too as she walked over to join the dozens of students huddled together under the large maple that stood halfway between Frame and Harvey Library. The kids were wearing an assortment of floor-dragging sweatpants and oversized Emerick College tops, the haphazard clothing worn by those rousted out of bed in the middle of the night. Every one of them was peering at a miniature screen, their fingers flying over the keypads.

"Who in the world are they communicating with at this ungodly hour?" Ruthalice wondered.

Deciding there was nothing nefarious in the excited chatter and texting generated by the night's drama, Ruthalice stepped back and began to walk. The only people who noticed her leave were pressed against the dark brick wall of Fox Hall, and even though the campus minister was well out of earshot, the couple stopped whispering and watched in silence until she disappeared into Jones Student Center.

Ruthalice turned right inside the glass-fronted lobby and started up the concrete steps to the "pub-flavored ambience" of the student hangout affectionately dubbed The Rat. Pausing to catch her breath, she surveyed the groupings of tables and comfy chairs strewn around the edge of the room. A shriek of dismay burst from the conversation pit directly in front of her.

"Oh, I'm so sorry. Oh my gosh, did you burn yourself? Are you all right?"

"Yes, Jen, I'm quite all right, thank you, just a little damp."

Ruthalice watched Evelyn Feller administer control and comfort simultaneously. "Way to go, Evelyn," she murmured.

The academic dean spotted Ruthalice and waved her over. "Please join us," she said, indicating the space beside her with an imperceptible nod. "We seem to have had a little accident," she commented gently as she accepted the wad of napkins the flustered coed thrust at her. "Do you know Jennifer Blake?"

Ruthalice smiled. "I don't believe we've met though your name is certainly familiar."

"Jennifer Blake, but uh, everyone calls me just plain Jen," she stuttered, still mortified by the great coffee spill incident. "I'm umm, Prissy's 'Little Sis.' I mean, Priscilla Brinkley." She looked miserably around the room. "We're, umm, both Delts."

Before Ruthalice could come up with a suitable reply, the carillon struck four times, followed immediately by a phone ringing next to her. Evelyn leaned against the cushioned sofa back and held her cell phone to her ear. "OK," she said wearily and struggled to her feet. As she clapped her hands, the handful of students scattered about The Rat raised their heads.

"The fire chief has just informed me the water pressure is back up in the dormitories, so you are free to use the bathrooms." Chair legs scraped as several of the young people took her up on the offer.

"I wonder where Priscilla is," Ruthalice muttered, as she watched Jen Blake follow the others down the stairs. "She strikes me as someone who wants to be in the thick of things, and this fire's the most excitement we've had on campus in years.

"Hmmm?"

"Oh, just curious why Jen's here without her roommate, Priscilla."

The dean shrugged. "My only contact with Ms. Brinkley is over academic issues." She glanced out the second story window at the orange-tinted night sky. "God, how I wish Babs were here. Throw anything academic you want to at me and I know exactly what to do, but I'm completely baffled by all the emotional histrionics which accompany episodes like this. That's why I insisted you come to campus, so you can blame me for the wakeup call."

Evelyn slipped her arms into the gray wool jacket slung around her shoulders and said pensively as they headed toward the stairs, "I hope I'm wrong about this, Ruthalice, but I fear we've only begun to feel the effects of this particular bonfire."

As the two colleagues walked down the cement stairs, knots of curious students untangled themselves from along the sidewalks and headed for the residence halls, leaving the rubber-suited fire fighters to mop up. The chief of police was holding court beside the Reflection Pool surrounded by college staff and a couple members of faculty.

Angus Bailey, director of facilities, stood at attention to Chief Turner's left like a well-trained soldier on review. President Richard Willson, his slim body silhouetted against the rotating lights of the emergency vehicles, stood beside the Oakes Quarry fire chief. Ruthalice drifted over to stand between Cliff and Charles. Evelyn joined the circle and gently took her secretary's arm.

"Mary," she whispered, "you really must take the day off."

"And leave you to cope by yourself?" Mary Scott leaned forward to catch the rest of the chief's instructions. "That's just plain ridiculous!"

"—So, no one is allowed to cross the police lines under any circumstances. I don't care who you are." Chief Turner aimed this last comment at Charles who, without warning, threw himself into the middle of the circle and glared at the police chief through bloodshot eyes. "This is unconscionable!" he shouted waving his arms. "I must have immediate access to the archives." Pounding his clenched fists against his thighs, Charles paced the space afforded him by the surrounding circle. The chief's right hand slipped down and unsnapped the cover of his swivel holster.

Ruthalice leaned into Cliff's side, a look of shock and dismay on her face. "Dear God, Curly is having a breakdown right here in front of everybody." Mesmerized by the spectacle unfolding before them, every member of the horrified little assembly waited for someone else to do something.

Then, as abruptly as the ranting began it stopped. The old professor seemed to wilt in front of their eyes as a look of abject sadness softened his face. "I simply must be allowed into Penington Place," he moaned, "to ascertain the extent of the damage to the archives."

"The building is still smoldering." Cliff stepped in front of him and placed both hands on his shoulders. A collective sense of relief swept around the little gathering. "I am certain you will be one of the persons allowed access to Penington Place as soon as the situation is under control." Cliff cast a meaningful look at Richard, who in turn glanced at Chief Turner, indicating the decision was not entirely his to make. "The sad truth is that whatever damage there is to the archives has already been done."

Shrugging off Cliff's words and his hands, Charles crossed the trampled grass and placed himself squarely in front of President Wilson.

"Charles," Richard began firmly, "we'll move as quickly as we can." He raised both hands to forestall any further onslaught. "That's all I can promise you at the moment."

With a grunt, Charles turned and hobbled away. Ruthalice winced as he stumbled across the grass.

"What on earth is wrong with him, Cliff?" Ruthalice whispered. "I've never seen Curly this worked up about anything. His behavior strikes me as way out of proportion to the loss of a bunch of old books."

"Which simply proves you're not a historian," Cliff shot back. Ruthalice flinched at the unexpected rebuke. "But I agree with you," he added quickly. "He is way out of bounds on this one." Cliff stuffed his hands into the pockets of his corduroy jacket. "But I doubt it matters what you and I, or anyone else around this circle thinks; Charles is determined to get inside Penington Place come hell or high water."

As the fire chief returned to his men, the impromptu staff meeting broke into private conversations. Picking their way over limp fire hoses, Dean Feller and her secretary were the first to leave.

"You know what? I'm starving." Ruthalice pulled up her sweatshirt sleeve and checked her watch. "Come on, we've got time for a Sausage 'n Egg McMuffin." She grabbed Cliff's hand and began dragging her less-than-enthusiastic spouse toward the parking lot.

"I always wondered who ate breakfast at a fast food joint this early in the morning," Ruthalice said as the M&Ms filed into the nearest McDonald's. "Now I know."

Twenty minutes later, Cliff tossed their grease-stained wrappers in the trash bin, then lightly touched his wife's shoulder. "We'd better head back. I've got to prepare for Invertebrate Lab this afternoon."

"Mollusk time again?"

"Yup," he sighed contentedly. "Now I get to really shine." He fastened the seat belt. "Are you staying on campus?"

"Absolutely." Ruthalice backed Lemon Drop with its "Follow a Friend to Emerick College" bumper sticker out of the parking space and headed back to campus.

## CHAPTER SEVEN

I n an attempt to be hospitable—*Sounds so much better
than "nosy,"* Ruthalice grinned to herself—she had
dropped by the Leaky Cup before heading to the
squad car parked in front of Penn Place. The occupant,
undoubtedly recognizing the Leaky Cup's signature
Santa Claus-red, cardboard sleeve with the tilted-mug
logo, ran the squad car window down to accept the
outheld gift. The brass ID bar pinned to the handsome
black woman's navy-blue uniform read ROSEMARIE
HARRIS. She popped off the plastic lid, took a cautious
sip, and grinned at her benefactor.

"I'm never one to pass up a cup of good, hot coffee.
Thanks."

"You're quite welcome." Ruthalice nodded at the
badge. "My name's Ruthalice, all one word, Michels.
My family calls me Ali, but around here I pretty much
insist that people use my full name."

Rosemarie nodded. "My folks call me Rosi with an
'i,' but everyone else calls me Lieutenant Harris, or just
plain Harris. I prefer Rosemarie myself."

"Mine's with an 'i' too. I'm the campus minister
here at Emerick."

With the introductory chit-chat out of the way,
the two women fell into easy conversation, until Ruthalice turned to the topic on both their minds this
smoke-scented Wednesday morning.

"May I ask what's your take on this fire, Lieutenant
Harris?"

"The preliminary report indicates it began in the basement. The state fire marshal will determine the exact cause." The officer's gaze followed the black streaks reaching up to the second story on the outside brick wall. "I expect there is significant smoke and maybe even water damage upstairs."

Rosemarie paused, wondering how much surmising was within bounds here. *I know all the regs against hypothesizing with the public,* she reminded herself, *but this gal's a minister. If you can't trust the minister these days, who can you trust?*

"Do you know what's in the basement?" she asked.

"As I recall there's not much down there, but I've only been in the basement a couple of times hunting for some old folder in one of the metal file cabinets." Ruthalice grimaced. "The last time I was down there was in the middle of a thunderstorm and all the power went out. I am here to tell you, Rosemarie, I felt like Tom Sawyer in that cave when their last candle burned out and it was so pitch black, Tom couldn't even see his hand in front of his face." The lieutenant watched Ruthalice shiver. "Each time the lights flickered back on I inched my way closer to the stairs and the light of day. For months I had nightmares of being trapped in the bowels of that darn basement."

The lieutenant wasn't about to admit she'd never read *Tom Sawyer,* or *Huckleberry Finn,* for that matter, though the Good Lord knew her mom had told her about them often enough.

"I gather there are no windows, right, so the only way in and out of the cellar is down a flight of stairs?"

"Correct. There's something interesting about that staircase wall though." Ruthalice paused and closed her eyes. "There's like a little cave in the wall, like maybe a third of the way down." The lieutenant looked up sharply.

"Is it big enough for a person to fit in?"

"I kinda doubt it, though I was never tempted to reach around inside. It's more like somebody cut out a rectangular cubicle in the cinder block wall." Ruthalice scratched her cheek. "I have heard Ernestine Perkins, our director of alumni relations who works on the second floor, tell visitors the head of school used it to store canned goods in pre-refrigeration days."

"So, nobody's in the basement now."

"Its sole use these days is to house files of ancient alumni records and discarded parlor furniture."

"And upstairs?"

"That's where the Quaker archives are housed. Since the college doesn't have an archivist per se, there's a part-time work student who staffs the desk a couple afternoons a week."

"So, what's the history of this house anyway?" Rosemarie arched her back against the vinyl seat and draped her hands over the steering wheel.

"Oh goody, I was hoping you would ask." Ruthalice assumed her best Quaker-tour-guide manner. "Hannah Elizabeth Emerick was our first head of school—this was during the Civil War days—and she lived in the Dean's House, as it was known then, during her six-year term. After Hannah's death the name was changed to Penington Place and, until five years ago, it was home to all the presidents. At that time, the trustees remodeled Penn Place into a hospitality center for receptions and alumni gatherings, stuff like that." Aware her companion was losing interest, Ruthalice concluded. "It *was* a wonderfully elegant spot for a tea party."

"Fire in a structure that old is often traced back to faulty wiring or a mouse chewing on something it shouldn't."

"That's what I thought until my husband reminded me that he served on the committee that oversaw a complete remodel of the entire structure." Ruthalice placed a hand on each knee for balance, leaned forward, and spoke through the open window. "Could this be arson?"

"That's up to the arson squad to determine," the lieutenant replied. "Mind if I change the subject?" She glanced up at Ruthalice who gave an encouraging nod. "My son Russell's a senior this year at OQ High. He's got his heart set on playing ball for the mighty Quakers next fall. Coach Adams told us Russ has an excellent chance of starting as offensive lineman."

"Hey, that's great! Have Russell look me up when he gets here. I'm partial to football players."

Russell's mom pulled her police cap over her black curls and opened the door. She lifted herself gracefully off the seat and leaned her slender body against the squad car. "Listen," she began handing the empty cup to Ruthalice, "I'm gonna be here the rest of the afternoon but don't you be bringing me any more coffee understand, 'cause if you do, I'm gonna have to find a place to pee!"

Ruthalice laughed, took the empty cups, and leaving Rosemarie to her solitary vigil, ambled back to her office.

# CHAPTER EIGHT

U nable to concentrate, Ruthalice straightened the jumble of pamphlets littering the top of the coffee table, watered the drooping hibiscus in front of the window, and was about to resort to dusting when she was saved from further puttering by a tentative knock. The sight of Rani in the doorway nearly took her breath away.

Dressed in iridescent blue, Rani's body glistened like royalty as she stepped into the room. What looked like purple and yellow blobs running along the hem and down the length of each sleeve were intricately embroidered flowers.

"Where on earth did you get that fantastic dress?" Ruthalice touched the cotton sleeve. "Those flowers look hand-embroidered. I can't even begin to fathom the amount of time and patience required to make something that exquisite. How many flowers are there?"

Rani's dark eyes beamed. "There are exactly ninety-three flowers. Each one took me fifteen minutes to embroider. The plant is the lignum-vitae, our Jamaican national flower. It was my project for senior sewing class." Her clear voice, uncharacteristically confident, dropped to a hush, as if she were suddenly afraid of succumbing to hubris. "I received a Highest Mark and was awarded a scholarship to continue my homemaker course for the rest of the year."

Knowing the gesture would embarrass the heck out of her young visitor, Ruthalice managed to resist the overwhelming urge to throw her arms around her. For a brief moment the two women relaxed into the simple pleasure of each other's company, then Rani seemed to crumble as she sank into the armchair.

"She said it would be spectacular and you could see it for miles around." Rani began gently tracing the flowers on her right sleeve with her left hand. "Did those girls set the Penn Place fire, Ms. Ruthalice? I'm so afraid that's what Priscilla and the other girl were talking about in the bathroom." Gasping for breath, she began to sob. "Oh, sweet Jesus, forgive me!"

Leaning forward Ruthalice touched Rani's sleeve, then firmly squeezed her arm. "This fire is not your fault, Rani Sequoia Brown." She relaxed her grip. "You do not need to ask God's forgiveness."

"My father uses my full name when I'm in trouble. My mother calls me Rani Sequoia Brown when she wants to say how much she loves me." Rani wiped her cheek with the back of her hand. "But I'm so frightened," she sobbed. "I saw one of those fire-starting people—what do you call them?"

"An arsonist. You call someone who starts fires on purpose an arsonist." Ruthalice studied her tear-streaked face. "Are you saying you saw an arsonist, and you think it was Priscilla?"

Rani dropped her head. "I couldn't see the face—it was too dark, and the head was hidden inside a hood."

"Too dark? Where were you when you saw this person?"

"In my room. When I can't sleep, I stand at the window. The campus looks so different in the dark." She sniffled and pulled a tissue from the box that was always available on the table. "I saw a figure darting between the bushes. It could have been Priscilla."

"OK now, Rani, listen to me. The very first thing the fire marshal is going to do is figure out what started this fire. That's his job, OK? It doesn't do any of us any good at all if we jump to conclusions."

"What will happen now?"

"I don't know," Ruthalice replied. "All I am sure of at this point is that it's not your responsibility to sort this whole mess out."

"I will try not to worry about this. And," she added lightly, "I promise not to play detective."

"Good," Ruthalice replied, knowing full well she was not about to make the same promise to her young confidante. "We'll get this episode behind us, and life on campus will get back to what passes for normal around here."

Reassured by her time with the college chaplain, Rani returned to her dorm room and opened the door, being careful not to bump her roommate's bed. During Rani and Sally Pratt's freshman year, Sally's father built a sleeping loft on one side of the room. Her mother added a chair and her best reading lamp from home. Rani had settled for the institutional furniture that came with the room. The porcelain vase her grandmother gave her for her sixteenth birthday stood proudly on the wooden dresser, flanked by two photographs of her parents. A large, hand-woven basket served as a laundry hamper. Every morning when her bare feet touched the rough hemp mat beside her bed, memories of home washed over her. But best of all was the large poster hanging on the wall at the foot of her bed. It was a photograph of Kingston, taken from one of the surrounding hills. Rani loved the fact her hometown appeared as inviting as any other city on earth, its congestion, poverty, and decaying neighborhoods invisible from that distance.

*I know you can't smell the sea from our window, Rani,* the poinsettia-covered gift tag read, *but now you can see it from your bed. Love, Sally*

There'd been other gifts that first semester. One afternoon when the weather turned cool, the girl who lived at the end of the hall dropped by. "My mother doesn't give a rip what I do with my stuff," she stated bluntly, thrusting two gorgeous Pendleton wool blankets into Rani's arms. "She's just relieved I'm out of the house, so I don't interfere with her social life."

"But I can't take these," Rani protested.

"Trust me, it's going to get cold and you're going to need these. Besides, I've got way more than I need." Priscilla Brinkley, with the dorm reputation of 'way wealthy and full of herself' added softly, "Besides, I want you to have them."

Smiling at the memories, Rani dropped her book bag on the desk, then placed both hands on her stomach as the butterflies returned. She walked to the open window and gazed at the yellow police tape fluttering in the gentle breeze. Unable to quell the growing apprehension, she turned around and noticed the blinking light on her wall phone.

"Hi, Rani, this is Luther." His rich Arabic-accented English stumbled with excitement. "Are you coming to the International Students' Club meeting tomorrow night? Hope you can stay afterwards. Call me, OK? Thanks, bye."

Luther Mouana and Rani Brown enrolled in Emerick College the same year and, as two of only a handful of non-white students, quickly became friends. Whenever Rani looked at his stick-thin body and deep-set eyes shining from a gaunt black face, she remembered the child running behind its mother she'd seen in a statue at the Cincinnati Freedom Center.

Rani lifted the receiver, punched the little squares, and informed Luther's answering machine she planned to attend the club meeting and would be pleased to stay afterwards. That task completed she rummaged through her backpack, opened the Western Europe history text and was soon lost in the gory battlefields of World War I.

# CHAPTER NINE

Relieved to discover it was almost four o'clock, Lieutenant Rosemarie Harris yawned and stretched until her hands pressed against the ceiling of her squad car. As the police radio crackled, she dropped her arms and reached for the handset.

"Harris, here." She listened intently then opened the door and hopped out of the car, relishing the crunch of dry leaves under her sturdy black shoes. "Ah, fall," she opined, walking the fifty yards to Penington Place. "We've even got the smoke to go with it."

She ducked under the yellow tape and crossed the porch, gingerly testing each board before trusting it with her weight. She peered through the opening where the battered front door had kept out the rain and snow for over a hundred years. Bracing herself with both hands, she leaned inside. Two charred lumps huddled together in the back corner were all that remained of a once-splendid pair of wingback chairs. Lt. Harris spotted the back door and the outline of a stove and refrigerator through two gaping holes in the wall between the kitchen and the front parlor.

As she surveyed the damage it suddenly occurred to her that she and Russell would never be invited to the traditional Tea with the President held in Penington Place on Parent's Weekend. Rosemarie Harris, the youngest of five children and a lifelong resident of Oakes Quarry, Ohio, had gone directly from high school to the Police Academy. The fact she had never once set foot on the campus of Emerick College campus until today did nothing to lessen her sense of loss.

"Funny how the thought of missing something I'd never even heard of before today makes me feel sad."

Rosemarie shook herself and began a quick tour of the outside, keeping an eye out for anything that looked out of place. The beige sandstone foundation blocks were warm to the touch. She had just rounded the corner at the back of the building when Chief Turner climbed out of his cruiser and marched across the lawn.

"Harris!" he barked.

"Chief."

"You're relieved. See you in the morning."

"So much for, 'Did you find anything suspicious, Lieutenant Harris?'" she grumbled under her breath as she headed to her cruiser. She started the ignition and was about to pull away from the curb when she saw a man careening toward her frantically waving his arms. She turned off the engine and opened the window while she ran a quick professional assessment: *suspect is mid-eighties; lives alone, therefore gets and does things his own way.*

"Officer," he gasped, placing both hands on top of the car while he caught his breath. "Officer, a word please."

*Add 'out of shape',* she thought to herself.

"It's urgent that I be allowed to assess the damage to the Quaker Archival Collection." He bent over and leaned into the open window. "Can you help me gain entrance to Penington Place?"

"Chief Turner's in charge of the investigation, sir. You'll have to check with him."

The head withdrew like a turtle into its shell.

"The chief is still inside the building!" she shouted as the old professor headed across the lawn. "What was that all about?" she wondered as she drove down Division Street toward the police station. "None of your business, girlfriend, your workday's finally over."

Ruthalice was halfway to her car when she witnessed the encounter between Charles and Lieutenant Harris. Doing an about-face, she ducked under the police tape, gingerly climbed the front steps, and peered inside. The late October sun barely penetrated the soot-covered windows. Ruthalice groped for the light switch and flipped it up. Nothing.

"Duh, what'd you expect, dummy?" She stepped inside and hollered, "Charles, it's Ruthalice. You still here?"

Ruthalice heard footsteps overhead and headed for the bottom of the stairs, cautiously circumventing the jagged hole in the center of the wooden floor. She braced her right shoulder against the wall and began to work her way up the steps.

"What are you doing here?" Chief Turner loomed above her at the top of the staircase.

Ruthalice flinched, then caught herself. "I don't think we've officially met, Chief. I'm Ruthalice Michels, the campus minister. I thought I saw Professor Hopkins come in here." She climbed the remaining four steps. "I share his concern for the condition of the archives, and—"

"He came and went." The chief ignored her outstretched hand. "As for you, young lady, you leave when I do, so make it fast."

Ruthalice did a quick scan of the archival room. Surrounded by high-back wooden chairs, the magnificent eight-foot marble-topped table dominating the center of the room appeared unscathed. Except for the strong acrid smell of smoke, the archival reading room was ready for its next researcher. She walked to the small desk under the window and picked up the green plastic nameplate: Priscilla Brinkley, Student Worker.

"OK," she said, tapping the sign against the palm of her hand, "that's why your name sounded so familiar."

"You coming?"

Since "No" was clearly not an acceptable answer, Ruthalice joined Chief Turner, who was waiting impatiently at the bottom of the staircase.

Chief Turner raised the yellow police tape as the two of them ducked under, then stopped in front of Ruthalice.

"I don't want to see you or that crazy professor of yours up there again, *comprendes?*"

"At least he didn't click his heels together," she grumbled as they went their separate ways.

## CHAPTER TEN

W hen Ruthalice got stuck behind a load of soybeans on Symmons Road, she was content to chug along at a steady 25 mph until the tractor finally pulled into a driveway, allowing the six-car lineup to zip on by. "I use the drive home to Horsefeathers Farm to decompress," she explained to a friend who asked if she regretted the commute. "I let the day's accumulated stuff assume its proper place in the larger scheme of life."

She stopped a quarter mile down Fair Ridge Road to collect the mail and newspaper from their respective boxes and drove up the hill.

"Unless there are some hotdog buns in the freezer I can nuke, it's beanie weenie time again," she told the empty garage. There weren't, but she did uncover a box of Stouffer's Macaroni and Cheese and half a bag of broccoli in the freezer door. "Good thing my sweetie's not a picky eater," she said, carrying her finds to the microwave. By the time Cliff arrived fifteen minutes later, the smell of cooking filled the house.

"Mmmmmm, that smells good. I figured we'd be making do with cereal tonight." He planted a kiss on her cheek. "Shall we finish the merlot?" Without waiting for a response, Cliff poured wine into two glasses and set them on the table. "Merlot and Macaroni Cheese," he stated, as Ruthalice set a plate in front of him. "Who says we M&Ms ain't suave and debonair?"

Rejoicing that this wonderful man came home to her every single night, Ruthalice dug into her supper. For the next ten minutes they ate in companionable and exhausted silence. It wasn't until after the plates were empty that either of them found enough energy to start a conversation.

"So, what did you learn from the policewoman?" Cliff laid his fork across his plate and burped. "I spotted you heading for the patrol car and figured you were about to ply her for information using a cup of the Leaky Cup's finest brew."

"Me? Plying information? Geez, Cliff, I was simply offering good old Emerick College hospitality." Ruthalice failed in her attempt to look aggrieved.

"OK, so what did you learn as a result of your good EC hospitality?"

"She spells her name with an 'I' also."

"And?"

"And she's at least relatively certain the fire started in the basement, though it will be a couple days before the fire marshal sends the final report." Ruthalice licked the back of her fork. "She was curious about that cubbyhole partway down the basement steps, the one Ernestine claims Hannah Emerick stored jars of canned food in during the summertime."

"What else did your policewoman have to say?" Cliff stacked the dessert and dinner plates, pinched the water glasses between his thumb and index finger, and stood up.

"First of all, she's not 'my policewoman.' Her name is Lieutenant Rosemarie Harris and she has a son named Russell who's planning to attend EC next fall and play football." Ruthalice yawned. "And that, dear Watson, is my report."

Cliff turned off the overhead and headed for the living room, leaving the dirty dishes in the sink. He sank into his Papa Bear recliner and reached for the remote.

"Ready for Game Three of the National League Playoff? I'm counting on not needing to expend an ounce of intellectual energy watching the Cubs and the Dodgers."

Ruthalice settled into her matching, forest-green recliner and wrapped the Ohio Bicentennial coverlet around her legs. The quilt was the gift of a grateful mother after the campus minister stayed with her son as he threatened suicide. Sufficiently shaken by their child's determination to leave school one way or the other, his parents said, "Do whatever you want to, son." The last time she saw Rudy he was happily tossing Caesar salads and stuffing chicken pot pies at the local Bob Evans.

"You know, Sweetheart, if you insist on lying down in that recliner, there's no chance you will make it past the second inning."

Cliff draped the pumpkin-covered afghan over his toes and pulled the remainder up to his chin. "You know me only too well," he said and blew her a kiss.

By the middle of the second inning with two outs and a man on third, the M&Ms were sound asleep. Neither of them saw the catcher clobber a home run into straightaway center field, putting the Cubbies ahead two to one.

# CHAPTER ELEVEN

A s evening slipped into night, Charles parked his cranky VW in the athletics parking lot and walked nonchalantly across Wood Avenue. Satisfied he had the backside of campus to himself, he made his way across the lawn.

"Take it good and easy, old boy," he counseled himself, grateful for the heavy clouds obscuring the moon. He paused under the black locust tree by the back porch and surveyed the campus again for signs of movement. Convinced campus security would not come this way for a good hour, he climbed the four steps and shoved the splintered back door open with his shoulder. He dug a pencil-sized flashlight out of the pocket of his tweed jacket, walked across the sticky linoleum floor, and shone the narrow, laser beam down the basement staircase.

"Got to do this one by yourself," he whispered, testing the top step with his left foot. The heavy smell of smoke and dampness engulfed him as he worked his way down the steps. He buried his face in his left arm as his body convulsed in a spasm of muffled coughs. With tears streaming down his cheeks, Charles finally felt the welcome cement of the basement floor. He pulled a handkerchief from his breast pocket, secured it across his nose and mouth—*like a damn Yankee cowboy*—and pointed his inadequate light at the stubborn darkness.

The old professor waved his left hand in front of his face as he shuffled forward, feeling the darkness with his fingers, the way he had as a lad in the dimly lit tunnels of the London Underground. When he reached the wooden wall separating the front two-thirds of the basement from the rear, he felt his way along the partition until his fingers found the door he was seeking. He lifted the metal latch and stepped into the old boiler room. Circumventing the original furnace, he stopped in front of the half wall of the coal bin and played the flashlight beam across the stone floor.

"Gideon's right. Everything's out, save his blanket pack."

Charles leaned forward, grasped the bundle with both hands and hoisted it over the waist-high partition. He knelt and ran his fingers over the rough woolen bundle. Inside he found a leather-bound Bible, a packet of loose-leaf lined paper wrapped in cellophane, and three ballpoint pens. Underneath a flannel shirt were a pair of trousers, one flip-flop, and some underwear. Suddenly uneasy pawing through another man's belongings, he tucked the blanket roll securely under his right arm, satisfied himself no trace of occupancy remained, and retraced his steps. Back upstairs he peered through the shattered kitchen window for a few minutes, before stepping out onto the narrow back porch.

The streetlamp in front of Harvey Library shone in both directions, but its light did not reach the backyard of Penington Place. Taking advantage of the dark spots afforded him, Charles reached his car and slipped inside just as campus security turned into the athletic facilities parking lot. He dropped the bundle on the floor between his feet.

"Hey, Professor Hopkins," the uniformed guard called, slowing down as he drove past. "Have a nice evening."

Charles gave a perfunctory wave, turned the ignition key, and drove the few blocks to Sheppard Place at a law-abiding 25 mph. He pulled into his one-car garage and waited until the garage door was firmly on the pavement, then walked into the kitchen.

He hung his coat on the hook behind the door. "It's me, Gideon," he called softly. "I've retrieved your belongings." He turned on the table lamp beside his favorite chair, creating a soft-yellow circle on the green carpet, laid the bundle on the floor, then sat down to wait. A slender, black man materialized in front of him. He lifted the soft bundle with both hands, smiled broadly, and bowed.

"Thank you, Professor Hopkins. You are my friend."

Gideon Boseka hunkered down on his haunches and began to unpack the frayed plaid blanket. Tucked under the clothes was a small square packet wrapped in a red bandana. He removed a wooden picture frame, a roll of dollar bills pinched in the middle by a blue rubber band, and a beaded necklace with a gold cross dangling from the middle. He raised the cross to his lips, then slipped the necklace over his head. Holding the photograph with his left hand, he touched the faces with his fingertips before placing the frame on the little square table beside Charles's chair. After meticulously counting the money, he nodded his approval and twisted the band around the bills before re-wrapping the roll in the bandana.

"My mother and my father and my little sister, Corinne." Gideon pointed to each face in the black and white photograph. "They are all dead now, Professor

Hopkins," he added, staring vacantly at the wall over the professor's right shoulder.

"You and I have much in common, my young friend." He studied the young man's face. "I survived the bombing of London by hiding in the Underground with hundreds of my countrymen. The Germans strafed our flat and killed both my parents. I was parceled out to my granny in the English countryside." Charles pointed at the harpsichord in the corner of the living room. "Do you see that picture, Gideon? That is my ma and my poppy. They are standing on the beach at Dover celebrating their tenth wedding anniversary. They were both dead two weeks later. It is the only photograph that survived the destruction of my home."

In one fluid motion Gideon rose and moved to the far wall. Bending over he squinted at the reddish-brown photo. "She is very pretty your mama, and your poppy he is very handsome." His entire face lit up. "We are both orphans—we are like brothers now—No, that is not right." A frown creased his forehead. "You are my uncle," he amended quickly. "Yes, Uncle Professor!"

Charles cleared his throat awkwardly, trying to banish unaccustomed emotions. "My friends call me Curly," he said. Gideon seemed to think for a moment.

"I do not wish to be disrespectful. Uncle Professor Curly?" he tried. "Too much. Professor Curly! That is good." Gideon resumed his seat on the carpet, his dark eyes darting anxiously around the room from object to object, as though any one of them might jump out at him. He ducked his head as the cuckoo clock began to chime. When the little brown, wooden bird finally reached twelve, the professor hauled himself to his feet.

"Gideon, my good man, I simply must retire." He rubbed his eyes. "Place your photograph and the rest of your belongings in your room."

Gideon sprang to his feet. "Tonight, I am safe in my new home," he said happily as he headed to the basement door. "Thank you, Professor Curly."

Charles stumbled into the bedroom at the end of the hall, kicked off his shoes, wrestled out of his jacket, and collapsed on the bed. He located the coverlet with his left hand, tugged it up over his shoulders, and turned off the light. Gideon waited until the professor began to snore. Finally reassured that all was well, he tiptoed down the wooden steps to his metal-framed cot in the unfinished basement.

Gideon dropped to his knees and closed his eyes. A lifetime of ducking and hiding and running taught him that safety is a relative term and sanctuary an ideal place which one never quite attains in this world. "No one has my back," he whispered. Forced to evacuate the burning building early the previous morning, Gideon had once again become the terrified young refugee escaping with his life. He fled to the one person he knew would offer shelter, at least for the time being.

"Gracious Father," he prayed, "cast me not away from thy presence and take not thy holy spirit from me." He touched the metal cot and ran his left hand over the soft blanket. "Two bed pillows, a warm duvet, and four clean towels! Thank you, sweet Jesus, thank you for my Professor Curly!"

Gideon pulled the black hooded sweatshirt over his head, climbed into bed, and entered the light sleep of one accustomed to being rousted out of bed in the dead of night.

On the west side of campus, Jennifer Blake was wrestling with demons of her own.

"Finally," she sniveled, sitting up in bed. She swiped at the tears running down her cheeks. "Where have you been?" She turned on the bedside light and whimpered, "I've been worried sick about you."

Priscilla glared scornfully in the general direction of the voice. "Who asked you to be my keeper?" She plopped down on the other bed and bent to untie her Nikes. "If you must know, Teddy and I had a date."

"But it's after midnight. You've been gone since *last night!*" Jen hated the way Priscilla always made her feel like an idiot for bothering to care. "That's more than twenty-four hours ago, Prissy!"

"Geez, my roomie's a mathematical genius!"

Jennifer crossed her legs and stared at her lap. She knew from past experience, if she waited long enough, there would eventually be some sort of explanation.

"We got a little high." Priscilla rubbed her forehead with the heel of her right hand. "And then Teddy had to have his snort, so he could tolerate the pain in his hand and relax. He's so worked up about being banned from even sitting on the bench with the rest of the soccer team. It's ridiculous." She unbuttoned her blouse. "By the time I got him chilled out, the damn campus was crawling with cops and fire fighters because of the fire." She fell backward onto the bed, her arms splayed wide on either side and yawned loudly. "The only smart thing to do was lay low, disappear someplace, and wait for the smell of booze and dope to just drift away." She fluttered her fingers in the air. "Satisfied?"

Jennifer felt sick to her stomach. She slid back down under the covers. "So, where'd you go?"

"The Holiday Inn, if it's any of your business." Priscilla propped herself up on one elbow. "Listen, Jen, shit happens sometimes, so don't get all stressed out about this fire, OK?" Her query was met with silence. "Teddy and I hung out around Fox Hall and kept a constant lookout. I can promise you, Jen, nobody went inside Penn Place last night. We can only thank God it was still too dangerous and hot."

"Is all this supposed to make me feel better?" Jennifer groused. She gazed at her roommate, who by now was snoring like a passed-out sailor. Jen buried her head under the pillow and willed herself to think about anything other than what had set off the Penington Place blaze.

# CHAPTER TWELVE

Thursday morning brought the first hard frost. Determined not to light the furnace until the end of the month, Ruthalice set bowls on the breakfast table, her plaid flannel bathrobe wrapped tightly around her.

"Our fire made the front page of the Out-County Section," Cliff announced as he folded the *Dayton Daily News* so he could read and eat simultaneously. "Let's see what we've got here."

Ruthalice poured two cups of coffee, assumed her customary place on the opposite side of the breakfast nook table, and leaned back against the vinyl cushion.

"Headline: *Historic building burns at local college.* 'A fire broke out early Wednesday morning at Emerick College, a small liberal arts school (founded by The Religious Society of Friends) in Oakes Quarry, fifty miles southwest of town. Penington Place, built in 1863 and designated a Historic Site in 1993 by the Ohio Historical Society, suffered extensive smoke and water damage.' Then there's the usual stuff about our heritage as an institution of higher learning dedicated to Quaker principles and testimonies, etc. etc. and—oh, listen to this: 'President Richard Willson is relieved to inform parents that no one was hurt.' Quote, Emerick students were never in danger, unquote. There's a file photo of Penn taken before the fire and another post-conflagration."

Cliff put a spoonful of Cheerios into his mouth and leaned into the newspaper. "Whoa, wait a minute! Hand me that magnifying glass would you, Ruthalice?" He waved his left hand in the direction of the stack of papers on her side of the table. "It's on the crossword puzzle."

Cliff peered at the photo. "Well, I'll be dad burned. What do you make of THAT?" He slid the newspaper and glass across the table.

"Exactly am I looking for?"

"Just look at the street."

Ruthalice brought the magnifying glass an inch above the police car parked beside the curb. A woman leaned against the vehicle apparently engaged in earnest conversation with the officer inside.

"It would appear that I'm married to a celebrity." Cliff leaned back and grinned broadly. "How many malacologists do *you* know whose wife's picture is featured in a major metropolitan newspaper? Social media's going to go viral with this."

"Oh, for pity's sake, Clifford, let's get real here. First of all, nobody can tell it's me except you. You can barely see my face, and besides, I was simply carrying out my pastoral care responsibilities, remember. And," she added, lowering her voice, "hoping for some hot not-ready-for-prime-time tidbits."

"Is there anything about arson," Cliff asked, as he dribbled honey on his English muffin. "That's your big concern, right?"

"It's clearly what Rani's most worried about." Ruthalice raised her chin enough to see through the lower portion of her bifocals and began to read: "Investigation into the cause of the predawn fire at Emerick College continues. Fire Chief Jacob Waters, interviewed at the scene, indicated the blaze began in the basement; probable cause is an explosion of undetermined magnitude. The Emerick College logbook indicates their security guard checked the outside doors of Penington Place at 12:30 a.m. and found them both locked."

Ruthalice removed her glasses and rubbed her eyes. "This whole story has an ominous ring to it," she said, putting her glasses back on. "How does it strike you?"

"I tend to agree, and I suspect the campus rumor mill is running in overdrive right about now." Cliff stood up and kissed his wife on the top of her head on his way to the sink. "Speaking of high gear," he said, glancing at the black-cat wall clock, "I've got to run." He stuffed keys and wallet into his pants pocket, grabbed his leather briefcase, and opened the mudroom door. "Have a good day, Sweetheart," he called over his shoulder. "Knowing you, I won't be a bit surprised if you've got it all figured out by suppertime."

"That's not going to happen," Ruthalice informed the hall of Mowry relatives on her way to the bathroom. She quickly brushed her teeth, then disappeared into the bowels of the master bedroom's colossal walk-in closet. She re-emerged five minutes later and finished buttoning a blouse lavishly strewn with raspberry and sky-blue orchids. Her trusty, all-purpose black skirt lay in a heap on the heirloom Windsor chair in the corner. She pulled it on, then stood in front of the dresser mirror. Using her fingers, she gently tugged the overnight knots out of her hair and began the French braid.

"This is so frustrating," she told the reflection. "I can't come up with a connection between Rani's bathroom conversation, a surprise twenty-first birthday party, and an explosion in the basement of Penn Place."

She flipped the braid over her shoulder. "What am I missing?"

Ruthalice made sure the front door was locked, grabbed her canvas bag off the kitchen counter, and headed for her car and the drive to campus. "My morning's wide open," she reminded herself as she pulled into the campus minister parking space, "and that means, if I get started right away, I've got plenty of time to poke around."

Ruthalice slung her bag over her shoulder and made a beeline for Penington Place. The lone policeman parked at the end of the cul-de-sac watched her approach. He climbed out of his black-and-white and stepped artfully between the campus minister and the bottom step of the front porch where he assumed the stance Ruthalice described as official police posture: legs three feet apart, weight solidly on the balls of both feet, hands on hips.

"This site's still under investigation, ma'am. You can't go in there."

Smiling brightly Ruthalice sneaked a surreptitious peek at his badge. *It looks like Doff but in this glare, for all I know that last 'f' might very well be a 't'.*

"I'm Ruthalice Michels, campus minister here at Emerick," she said brightly, extending her hand. The young officer shook it with little enthusiasm. "I spoke at length with Lieutenant Harris yesterday." She paused, hoping the age-old tactic of name dropping would improve her chances of being given some slack.

"All's I know, ma'am, is I've been instructed not to let anyone in the building until the chief gives the thumbs up." Anticipating her next question, he added, "And I don't know when that will be, ma'am."

*Darn, so much for Plan A. It's on to Plan B.*

"Can I bring you a cup of coffee, Officer Doff?"

"No thanks, ma'am. I don't drink coffee." A hint of a smile softened his face. "That's Dorft actually." Relaxing for an instant, he added, "They left the 'r' out of my name. The bursar claims she couldn't read my handwriting." His blue eyes seemed to focus on a distant memory. "The next order for badges goes in at the end of the month, so in the meantime I'm stuck with Doft."

"OK, Officer Dorft. I guess there are times when we've just got to live with the mistakes of others."

"Ain't that the truth, ma'am, but it can be a damn nuisance in the meantime."

Ruthalice waited to see if Officer Dorft, when he finished blushing, was going to elaborate, but he remained motionless, staring across the damp lawn at Dalton Science Hall.

"Well, I guess I'll move along, then. Have a nice day."

Ruthalice set a leisurely pace along the back wall of Penn Place, pausing to stare at the kitchen door. The yellow strip of tape affixed to the newel post sagged across the steps and out across the back lawn. Ruthalice picked up the loose end and wrapped it back around the trunk of the ash tree. Chief Turner pulled to the curb just as she came around the corner of the building. Unwilling to push her luck any further, Ruthalice followed the red brick sidewalk back to Frame Meetinghouse.

# CHAPTER THIRTEEN

"I've read the entire *New York Times,*" Charles said. He swallowed the last of his second cup of tea and set the cup back in its saucer. He checked his wristwatch. "My God, it's nearly ten o'clock," he grumbled. "Is this boy going to lie about until noon?"

Hearing the basement toilet flush, he slid out of the oilcloth-covered dinette chair and hollered down the stairs.

"Gideon, are you finally up?"

"Yes, Professor Curly," came the sleepy reply. "You want me to come up?"

"Yes, yes. I'm dreadfully late," he sputtered. "Should have been on campus an hour ago."

Massaging his temples with the heels of both hands, Gideon climbed the stairs and followed his host into the kitchen.

"Here," Charles said, thrusting a mug of tea into the young man's hands, "You and I must talk." Gideon wrapped both hands around the warm cup and stared at the contents. "Sit down, Gideon. You're making me nervous hovering around like that."

Charles leaned against the kitchen sink. "Listen, Gideon, the reality of our situation dictates we be very circumspect in our movements right now." He frowned in the general direction of the dinette table. "You've got to lay low for a few days until this damnable fire investigation is over."

Gideon frowned. "What is this 'lay low,' Professor Curly?"

"It means you are not to go outside or answer the phone or the door under any circumstances."

A look of alarm skittered across Gideon's face. "What about my job? I do not want to lose my job, Professor Curly."

"Bloody hell! You didn't say anything about a job!" The professor pulled out a chair and sat down heavily. "Where are you working?"

Gideon's head dropped. "At the warehouse out there." He pointed vaguely toward the window with his left index finger.

"Speak up, Gideon. I can't hear a word you're saying. Remember, I'm an old man."

Without raising his head, Gideon tried again. "At the home improvement store. I sweep the floor and stock shelves. I work three nights a week."

Charles stared in disbelief. "And no one's ever questioned you?"

"Never. I fill out a form and get job two weeks ago." His confidence restored, Gideon raised his head. "I save my money and go to Twin City!"

"Twin City? Oh, you mean Minneapolis-St. Paul." A soft smile replaced the grimace on Charles' face. "You know, Gideon, it's mighty damn cold in the Twin Cities in the wintertime."

Gideon hugged the mug of tea against his chest with both hands, his half-closed eyes hiding whatever he was thinking.

"Oh, never mind." Charles glanced at his watch. "What matters now is that you stay put, lay low, whatever."

Gideon opened his mouth to respond, but Charles cut him off.

"Listen, Gideon. Your presence in this house is going to land both of us in a heap of trouble. We dare not risk being run to ground."

Still unsettled, Charles rose to his feet and began to rinse his cup and saucer. "By the way," he said, taking a deep breath, "Who is your supervisor at the warehouse?"

"Miss Green. She's the boss lady. She come in at four o'clock every morning."

"So, this Miss Green, she'd be at the store now?"

"I think so." Gideon stared earnestly at his host. "She wants me to stock shelves on Saturday. What should I do?"

Charles slipped his arms into the black London Fog hanging beside the kitchen door and settled it over his worsted blazer. "It's only Thursday, Gideon," he replied, "which gives me a couple of days to figure a way out of our muddle."

He smiled at the young man seated at the table, his boney elbows propping up a narrow chin in his hands. In baggy pajama bottoms and a bright orange Bengals sweatshirt at least two sizes too big, Gideon looked as though the softest spring breeze would knock him down, but Charles knew otherwise.

"I'll be home for supper, Gideon. Remember, you are quite safe here as long as you remain undetected." Charles blinked and looked at his feet, surprised and embarrassed by an upsurge of unaccustomed emotions.

"I trust my friend, Professor Curly," Gideon replied, as his face broke into his million-dollar smile. "OK, I will, what you call it, stay put."

Gideon waited until his benefactor backed out of the garage onto Sheppard Street, then walked down the narrow hallway into the living room. He lifted a corner of the poplin drape and followed the professor's progress until he disappeared from sight. He watched a young mother pushing a cherry-red baby carriage past the house until she too disappeared around the corner. Across the street, a lanky, black-and-tan German Shepherd accompanied an elderly gentleman halfway down the block, then waited patiently while his master stooped to tie his shoe. Five minutes later the worn poplin curtain dropped silently back into place.

Ruthalice began her workday in the campus minister's office responding to Richard's request to prepare a tribute to Penington Place for a short commemoration Friday at noon.

"I want a combination of the important role Penn Place has played in the life of the college, a list of current use, activities, and programs housed in the building, interspersed with tantalizing historical tidbits. Can you say all that in a ten- to fifteen-minute reflection speech?"

"I think so," she assured the president. "Do you want a prayer as well?"

"Of course, that's a given."

By eleven-thirty, satisfied with the results of the morning's effort, Ruthalice reviewed her teaching notes for Friday's class on the Book of Joshua. She laid the CD with her favorite rendition of *Joshua Fit the Battle of Jericho* on top of the notes and closed her eyes. *Despite a multitude of human frailties and shortcomings, Yahweh led and delivered his people into the promised land.*

"And, God, please lead me in the right direction, so I don't get going in circles with this whole Penington Place debacle."

Ruthalice opened her eyes and stared at the reprint of her favorite Monet, which hung above her desk. Clear water played with the reflection of a small, brown boat floating on its surface. She could not remember how many times she'd longed to trade places with the calm figure sitting in the dinghy and trail her own fingers in the pond, imagining the melodic call of French birds hidden in the trees.

Her growling stomach interrupted the reverie. "Someone once said, 'Eat enough and it will make you wise.'" Ruthalice spun her desk chair around and got to her feet. "I'd say it's time to go and test that theory."

After lunch, since Ruthalice had to walk around Penington Place to get back to Frame Meetinghouse, she decided to take another look at the rear wall. Finally convinced there was nothing her untrained eye could learn by gawking at the smoke-streaked wall, she turned to leave, just as a large marmalade cat emerged from behind the nearest shrub. The cat paused for a moment, twitched its tail, and slunk behind the adjoining bush. Curious, Ruthalice stepped between the bushes for a closer look and caught a glimpse of black metal in the sandstone blocks. She dropped to her knees, reached out her right hand, and ran her fingers around the metal coil of a cast iron handle.

"I'll bet that's a door into a coal bin like the one we had in our basement."

After her parents bought the yellow stucco house on Lincoln Avenue, her father converted the huge coal burning furnace with its octopus-arms air ducts to natural gas. Every time it was Ruthalice's turn to fold laundry, her best friend, spooked by the ominous noises emitted by the boiler, insisted they bring the clothes up to the kitchen "where it's totally safe."

Chuckling at the memory, Ruthalice placed both hands against the sun-warmed stones and pushed herself to her feet. "Whew, I gotta pee," she announced to no one in particular. A silver Mercedes pulled into the empty parking place next to the spot reserved for the Campus President, and a familiar figure emerged from the driver's seat. Ruthalice sent a prayer of protection to the second floor of Fox Hall and headed for the ladies' room.

## CHAPTER FOURTEEN

Richard heard Sid Cope's arrival well before the knock on his office door. He straightened his tie, then adjusted his shirtsleeves until they covered his wrists. Resolved to soldier through this interview with as little damage to himself and the college as possible, Richard got to his feet.

"Come in, Sidney."

Sid Cope extended a well-manicured hand, then dropped into the chair occupied a few hours earlier by Dean Feller. "Damn shame about old Penn Place burning, Richard. I remember interviewing the head of PR in the parlor when I was a student in the eighties."

"I'd forgotten that public relations used to be in Penington," Richard replied, content to let Sid set the pace for their conversation. "You graduated cum laude in, what, eighty-five, if I remember correctly."

"Yes sirree, the class of 1985, all 115 of us. I prided myself on knowing everyone's name." His face lit up. "We played one heck of a game of football back then." As the most successful quarterback—both on and off the field—ever to wear the green and gold for Emerick College, Sidney R. Cope claimed his right to boast.

Well aware any word of encouragement on his part would result in a lengthy recitation on the glory days of Quaker football, Richard said nothing. His visitor guzzled his coffee, then tossed the Styrofoam cup into the wastepaper basket beside the president's desk.

"Yes. The old boy's still got it," he crowed.

Richard shifted in his seat, pulled up his left sleeve and pointedly consulted his watch.

"But, that's for another time." Sidney crossed his legs. "It's about this business with my nephew and Coach Stevens. I don't like it, Richard. First, Coach kicks Ted off the team for a goddamn accident, so the kid threatens to withdraw from school and run home to mommy." His angry recitation turned to scorn. "I thought this was a Quaker institution—all lovey-dovey and forgiving and crap like that. Whatever happened to supporting our athletes, forgive and forget?"

Momentarily taken aback by the invective, Richard fought the urge to wipe his face. As the verbal barrage ceased, he regained his composure.

"Bob Stevens has a good reason for everything he does, Sidney, and furthermore, I trust his judgment when it comes to team discipline." The president paused, braced for another outburst. When none was forthcoming, he continued.

"Theodore's a good kid and an outstanding goal-keeper. I suspect he's feeling pretty miserable about this whole incident. Some kids deal with their disappointment by, as you put it, 'running home to mommy.' Other than the fact that Theodore is one of our first-generation college students, I don't know any of the family dynamics. I do know that for some of our students, college is a daunting experience fraught with what often feel like insurmountable obstacles."

Sid Cope gazed impatiently out the window.

"Yeah, yeah, I know all that, Richard." He turned and fixed his steel-blue eyes on the president's face. "My brother, RJ, thinks this college stuff is a total waste of money. I suspect he's actually been waiting for his boy to hit the wall, come to his senses, and get his butt back to the farm where he belongs."

Sidney Cope clasped his hands and leaned forward, resting his elbows on the arms of the chair.

"I talked with Stevens yesterday afternoon, as a matter of fact. He told me about the bar fight." He rubbed the carpet under his chair with his right foot. "In other words, the true story." Choosing his words carefully, he went on. "Theodore's version of how he broke his hand is a bit creative." Sid snorted and shook his head. "Kids!"

Richard watched the transformation from in-your-face rage to unaccustomed disappointment. The transformation reminded him of an inner tube grown soft from a slow leak.

"My sister-in-law's the one who's most upset. She's keen on their oldest child going to college, 'to set a good example for the rest of the kids,' as she puts it." Cope shook his head. "Somehow Emma managed to persuade Roger to let Ted give Emerick a try, but now—"

Sid shifted his weight to his left hip and re-crossed his legs.

"My little brother only knows part of the story. Sometime Monday morning Ted called his mother. Emma immediately got hold of me and begged me to do something." His eyes softened. "My sister-in-law's one of those solid, down-to-earth gals you can bet the farm on. I've never seen that wonderful woman so upset, which is precisely why I came by today." He paused and vigorously rubbed the tip of his nose with his right index finger. "To do something about it."

"Has your nephew already withdrawn?"

"Not yet. His mother and I treated him to a Bob Evans' meal this morning. As of eleven o'clock, he's agreed to stick it out at least until the end of this semester. I extracted a promise from Stevens that if Ted stays in shape, he'll put him back in goal next fall." Sidney straightened up to his full height. "He will be ready. I assured Coach I would take personal responsibility for his conditioning."

"So, I take it Theodore remains here at Emerick on his uncle's nickel. That's mighty generous of you, Sidney." Richard felt himself begin to relax for the first time in two days. "Am I to assume the true story of how Ted broke his hand remains between his mother, his coach, and his uncle?"

Sidney Cope snorted. "The whole team sure as hell knows, you and Dean Feller know. Rumors have made the rounds all over campus, but yeah, other than that, only his mother and I know!" Cope looked at the president and shrugged. "But, hey, that's life on a small campus, right? Some things may have changed since my day, but you can be damned sure the old rumor mill is still churning out the really good stuff."

"Ted tells me the campus minister talked to him. I reminded him that confession's good for the soul even if the woman's only a Quaker and not a Catholic priest. No offense, Richard," he added hastily.

"None taken, Sidney." The two men got to their feet. "Ruthalice Michels is a very perceptive listener. I hope your nephew will talk with her again." Richard reached for the knob as his secretary's gentle knock signaled his next appointment had arrived. "I'm pleased you found a workable solution, Sidney," he said, extending his hand. "Let's see if we can find a golf date the next time I'm out your way."

"Oh, that reminds me." Cope reached into his breast pocket and extracted a fistful of Ohio State basketball tickets. "Opening game of the season," he said. "A present from Cope Sporting Goods, compliments of the management." He pressed them into Richard's hand. "Distribute these however you wish."

And with his habitual, we're-all-in-this-together wink, Sidney Cope walked out the door. Richard and his secretary, Lynn Lawson, stood, side by side, watching him wend his way down the hallway and disappear into the elevator. The president took a deep breath and looked around for his next appointment.

"Here she comes." Lynn nodded toward the co-ed jogging down the corridor from the nearest restroom. "Her name's Roxanne Dubois."

"OK, and what's on her mind?"

"Roxy, as she prefers to be called, addressed the faculty meeting last April about the college's moral obligation to speak out against the Iraq War."

"Ah, yes, now I remember. Not shy about sharing her opinions, is she?"

"No comment," his secretary replied softly, returning his smile. "But today she says she wants an interview for the student paper about the fire."

"Ah, Roxanne, please come in. I understand you want to talk about the unfortunate fire in Penington Place." Richard's voice trailed off as he shut the door.

"President's office," Lynn said, answering the ringing phone. She listened for a moment, then nodded silently. "Yes, sir, I'll be sure to tell him. Thank you for calling."

## CHAPTER FIFTEEN

Professor Hopkins presented a decent lecture titled "The Rise and Fall of Mayan Civilization" to his two o'clock senior History of the Americas seminar and wandered back to FH 207. Gazing around his cluttered office, Charles felt like a shuttlecock being bandied back and forth over the badminton net. One minute he was confident, trusting his innate ability to discern where he was going, the next step clearly in view. A moment later, he was immobilized, frightened by the potential cost if he made a mistake.

"Why me?" he asked the empty room. He heard his granny's voice. "Why not you, Charlie? Who else can the boy run to? Who else will shelter him?"

Charles grunted. "That's not fair of you, Granny." He leaned against the windowsill and studied the charred walls of Penn Place. "I didn't even know you were here."

Turning his back to the window, Charles picked up the heavy receiver of his landline desk phone and dialed.

"Yo!" said a strong male voice.

"Is this Luther?" After a quick introduction, Charles delivered his request. "An old friend showed up at the house the other night. The two of you have some things in common, and I'd like you to meet him. Therefore, please accept this invitation to drop by my house this evening."

"I have the International Club Meeting at seven pm—" came the startled reply.

"Luther, my request is relevant to your work as an international student, specifically as an African student. Let me assure you that honoring my invitation will be an extremely valuable use of your time. In fact," he added, pleased he'd thought of the idea, "will you join us for dinner?"

"That is not necessary, Professor Hopkins. I will take my meal in the cafeteria, and I will be at your home this evening as you have requested."

"Thank you, Luther."

Relieved his persistence had paid off, Charles hung up, picked up the volume lying open on his desk, and began to read. A moment later, a loud knock on the door made him jump. President Wilson and Dean Feller grinned at him through the doorway.

"Didn't mean to startle you, Charles," Richard said, apologetically.

"That's quite all right. To what do I owe this auspicious interruption?"

"Evelyn and I are on our way to meet Chief Turner. Knowing your deep concern about the condition of the Quaker Archives, we thought you might like to join us. Can't promise we'll be able to go upstairs yet, but you're welcome to come along."

"Jolly thoughtful of you, Richard." Standing and placing the open volume face down on his desk, Charles stepped around the desk and accompanied them down the steps onto the sidewalk. "Has a cause been determined yet?" he asked.

Richard spotted Chief Turner standing stiffly on the front porch of Penington Place, a female officer by his side. "That may be one of the things the chief wants to talk with us about."

Pat Turner removed his hat and dark glasses as the little trio joined him on the porch.

"I believe you all know Lieutenant Harris." Evelyn offered her hand and smiled. The men nodded as the chief outlined the plan. "OK folks, we'll take a quick tour of the building, so you can see the extent of the damage. We will need a secure place to sit and go over the department's final report after the tour."

Charles rubbed his sweaty palms together before shoving his hands into his pockets, praying no one noticed his nervousness.

"We'll begin upstairs," the chief announced, leading the way.

The little entourage dutifully followed in single file, Evelyn, Richard, and Charles all maintaining a respectful distance from the wobbly banister. Lieutenant Harris, whose assignment was to "keep a professionally inquisitive eye on these college muckety-mucks," brought up the rear.

Dean Feller stopped the procession halfway up to gaze at the scene below.

"A sad sight I'm afraid, isn't it, Evelyn?" Richard said. "The trustees will have to determine whether the old gal is restored or torn down."

Evelyn dug a handkerchief out of her pocket and quickly wiped her eyes before climbing the rest of the stairs. The little company moved into the center of the archival room, each member burdened with their own disquieting thoughts and sense of loss.

"As you can see, this area suffered extensive smoke damage." Chief Turner turned to face the president. "Your facilities people need to lay plywood over the holes in the parlor floor and repair this railing. Your staff must also cover and secure the doorways before anybody is allowed up here to do anything. Understood?" The chief made eye contact with each one of them.

"Understood," Richard replied, conferring the official stamp of approval to the police chief's conditions. "I'll have Angus Bailey get boards down this afternoon."

"Good. Once those safety measures have been taken care of, you may begin assessing the condition of these files and books. You're in charge up here, right, Professor Hopkins?"

Charles shuffled his feet. Richard quickly jumped in. "Professor Hopkins is the college's senior faculty member, and because his field is history, he's nominally in charge of this collection."

"Whatever," the chief replied with a shrug, recognizing departmental wrangling over turf when he heard it. "All right, then. We'll take a look at the kitchen, and then we're done with the onsite investigation."

"That sounds fine," Richard said. He turned to Charles. "What do you think, Charles?"

Charles looked startled. "Apologies, Richard," he added, seeing the puzzled look on the president's face. "I was thinking about the cellar." He turned to Police Chief Turner. "Has anything been found in the basement to explain the cause of this unfortunate fire?"

Turner replaced his police hat, then tugged on the brim, settling it firmly on his head. "We've got probable cause. I'll explain further when we have privacy," he added, looking directly at the president.

"Yes, of course." Richard glanced at his watch. "Let's head up to my office. I'll call my secretary and order beverages and sandwiches sent up." He touched Charles lightly on the shoulder. "Charles, I'll be giving a full report to the faculty as soon as I have something specific to share, but for right now, this conversation needs to stay at the President's Council level."

Attempting to appear cool and unperturbed, Charles said briefly, "I understand," and, nodding jerkily to the others, turned and headed down the stairs.

After an uncomfortable pause, Richard turned to Rosemarie and asked, "Will you be joining us, Lieutenant?"

"Officer Harris will be with us," Chief Turner replied. "She has an observation that's pertinent to this investigation."

"Shall we adjourn to my office, then, gentlemen, ladies?"

Lieutenant Harris brought up the rear as they headed back to Fox Hall. She glanced over her shoulder and spotted the campus minister, evidently holding an animated conversation with herself as she crossed the porch of Frame Meetinghouse.

"Hi, Ruthalice with an 'i,'" Rosemarie whispered. "It's reassuring to know at least one person on this campus isn't so full of themselves they're afraid to open their mouth for fear of looking the uneducated fool."

Flooded with rage and disappointment, Charles stalked toward his car. "Damn and double damn," he snarled as he reached his car, kicking the tire, for want of a better target. "Tossed aside like a leaky, old bucket!"

Still furious at his abrupt dismissal from the meeting with the police, Charles stopped at the hardware store on his way home, selected the brightest flashlight on the shelf, added two packs of D batteries, and headed to the checkout counter. Ignoring the "Have a nice day, sir" from the twenty-something clerk, he stuffed himself into the battered VW and drove home.

He lay his purchases on the kitchen table, and whistling softly to announce his presence, wandered into the living room. The last rays of sunlight fell on Gideon's back as he sat on the loveseat, a Bible open in his lap.

"Good evening, Professor Curly." He placed a thin, index finger on the well-worn page. "Was it a good day, today?"

"Hello, Gideon. It will be a better day with some sherry." He uncorked a bottle of Dry Sack, poured half a glass, and raising his glass toward Gideon, exclaimed, "Cheers!" He took a swallow and a long satisfied 'ahh-hhhhh' slipped out as he held the glass gently between his fingers and thumb. "I'm sorry you will not join me in a drink this evening."

Gideon ran his finger up and down the page before shutting the Bible and placing it on the cushion beside him. As he realized Gideon hadn't moved a muscle since closing the book, Charles swallowed the lump growing in his throat.

"Well," he said as he set the sherry glass on the table beside his chair, "I have what I hope will be a pleasant evening in store for us tonight." Except for a quick brightening in his eyes, Charles thought he might as well be talking to a deaf man. "Are you aware there is a student at Emerick from Chisimaio?"

Gideon's thin body shifted on the cushion as he leaned forward a fraction of an inch. "No, I did not know this. What is his name, Professor Curly?"

"Luther Mouana. He's a junior and a biology major." When Gideon's expression did not change, Charles looked at the floor to hide his disappointment. "I was hoping you would know him."

"Somalia is a big country." A ghost of a smile touched Gideon's mouth. "I have some family on my mother's side called Mouana, but because of civil war in our country, I do not see any of them since I was a child."

"I have invited Luther to join us at seven o'clock." He raised his head. "I thought you might enjoy conversing with a fellow countryman after spending these past five months in that dank coal bin with no one to chat up."

Feeling slightly chilled, Charles lifted the discarded cardigan from the back of his armchair and draped it around his shoulders before sitting down. Gideon remained motionless as he watched his benefactor from across the room.

"I have not talked with a Somali since Serita died." He closed his eyes for a moment, a shadow of grief resting on his face.

"I remember Serita quite fondly. Such an enchanting woman and so charming at your wedding." He stopped unsure how much more reminiscing was appropriate.

"It was a short marriage, only two years." Gideon briskly rubbed his hands together as though he, too, were chilled. "Now I cannot become an American citizen because my American wife is dead." A note of bitterness crept into his sorrow. "I must hide underground so INS not send me to my death in Somalia."

"Damnably rotten this US policy, isn't it, old chap." Charles swallowed the sour taste in the back of his mouth. "I've said it before, and I'll say it again, it's a rotten way to run the country where Lady Liberty proclaims bring me your huddled masses, your tired and your poor!"

Gideon shrank against the back of the couch. "All I want is to breathe free air in America, but now I huddle and hide and run again."

The doorbell rang as the purple martin warbled seven times from the bird clock in the kitchen.

"Our guest has arrived." Charles got to his feet. "Come, we shall welcome Luther Mouana to our humble abode."

# CHAPTER SIXTEEN

With their meeting over, Richard accompanied the police officers to the bottom of the stairs. The campus security lights hummed and flickered to life as they were shaking hands.

"You've put in a long day, Chief Turner. I'm grateful to you and Lieutenant Harris for your time."

"Glad to be of service, President Willson. That's what the townspeople pay us to do." Turner stepped onto the pavement, then turned and added, "I'll get that written report to you in the morning."

Richard leaned against the sun-warmed brick wall, content to survey his beleaguered domain as the officers drove away. A boisterous group of male students swaggered down the walk on their way to the brightly lit playing field. "Oh, that's right," Richard muttered, "This is Theodore's first night of probation." Richard pushed himself off the wall with his elbows and went inside.

He stuck his head through the doorway of the academic dean's office. "Still here, I see."

Dean Feller looked up from the files on her secretary's desk. "Just checking on Mary's progress with those student academic difficulty alert forms." She straightened up. "You look exhausted, Richard. I hope you're on your way home."

"I am—going home, that is—and exhausted."

She thought his smile looked incredibly sad. "What do you make of the broken lantern by the old original furnace?"

"I'm not sure," he replied. "It does seem an unlikely place for a campout, doesn't it?"

She nodded and took a step toward him. "When will you issue a formal statement to the college community?"

"The minute I receive the written police report, I'll call the Council together."

Dean Feller watched her boss wander back toward his office, relieved he had shown no inclination to discuss the situation further. Richard's tendency to think things through before sharing them with her often drove her nuts, but tonight Evelyn was grateful to be by herself.

She drove down Wood Avenue to her condominium, unlocked the unit's front door and stepped into the foyer. "My programmable bread machine comes through again," she sighed, inhaling the fragrant smell of freshly baked bread. She sighed and slipped off her shoes. "Black bean soup, French bread, and a glass of wine. Not a bad way to spend the evening."

A half hour later, she advised the *Jeopardy* contestants, "No, not who is Socrates. Who is Alexander the Great?" She set her empty bowl on the TV table and raised her wine glass. "To an uninterrupted evening, Mr. Trebek."

She got her wish, and by eight-thirty, the academic dean of Emerick College was sound asleep in her chair.

# CHAPTER SEVENTEEN

The terrified little girl dove under the empty, cardboard boxes at the back of the alley and held her breath as dark figures loomed above her hiding place, kicking boxes, shouting, and swearing, "Come out, come out wherever you are! You little bitch!"

Rani sat bolt upright in bed, shaking uncontrollably. Pulling the blanket to her chin, she gasped for breath, grateful for the streetlight leaking around the heavy draperies.

"You OK, girl?" Her roommate raised her head.

"I was having an awful dream, that's all."

"Oh dear, not again, Rani. I'm so sorry." Sally rolled over. "What time is it, anyway?"

"It's only 5:30. I'm all right, really I am. You can go back to sleep."

Rani sank back into her pillow, relieved she didn't have to put the reoccurring nightmare into words. Determined to keep the terror at bay, Rani focused on Luther Mouana.

She knew it wasn't like him to forget an International Club meeting. Something unexpected must have happened. She drew her knees up, untucking the blankets from the end of the bed.

*I should have taken Sally's advice and asked for a tall mattress,* she sighed, annoyed at her reluctance to assert herself. *This bed's too short!*

Remembering Sally's well-intentioned advice their freshman year, Rani closed her eyes and smiled. "You ought to try out for basketball," Sally had said, quick-

ly sizing up her new roomie's six-foot-one-inch frame.
"The Lady Quakers are desperate for women over five-
and-a-half feet who are coordinated and can run and
shoot!"

Rani threw off the blanket, still embarrassed by her
curt response. "I came to the US for a college education
and to complete my teacher training, not to play ball
games. I plan to graduate and return to Kingston where
I will open the Friendly Little Red School and invite
all the street ragamuffins wandering the alleys of my
neighborhood to come to school."

It took three months sharing a room with her before Rani realized just how much she admired Sally
Pratt. As she sat in bed listening to her roommate's
gentle snoring, Rani imagined the rest of her daydream
plan: She would invite Sally to come and teach the children how to solve their disagreements without hitting
each other.

Smiling to herself, Rani grabbed her towel and cos-
metics case and headed for the bathroom. In the relaxing heat of the shower, she revisited last night. When
Luther didn't show up as expected in her dorm's downstairs lobby, she walked over to the Leaky Cup thinking
she had misunderstood, and he was planning to meet
her over there. However, when she arrived, the coffee
house was empty except for five women sharing a textbook at the oval table in the middle of the room. When
she got to the International Club meeting, no one knew
where Luther was or why he hadn't come.

Back in her room, Rani decided she needed to be
assertive. She took a deep breath and dialed Luther's
room.

"Yeah?"

"Luther?"

"Yes."

"This is Rani. Do you want to have breakfast with me?"

"I can't, Rani. I've got class."

"This is Friday, Luther. You don't have an eight o'clock class on Fridays." Rani was determined to see this through. "Did you forget we were going to meet at the Leaky Cup last night?"

Her query was answered by labored breathing, then a painful swallow.

"Luther are you sick?" she asked, suddenly alarmed. "You sound like you don't feel well."

"I don't feel well, Rani. I was up until five this morning. I had just fallen asleep when you called and woke me up." Luther cleared his throat. "Rani, I gotta go. I'll call you later."

"What was that all about?" Sally rolled over in bed, her mousy brown hair sticking out in tiny spikes.

"Oh, nothing."

"Nothing?" Sally regarded her skeptically. "If I had to guess, I'd say you got stood up last night."

"Luther asked me for a coffee before the IC meeting, but he never showed up." Rani watched her roommate's face in the full-length mirror nailed to the closet door. "I suggested we have breakfast, but he says he doesn't feel well. I'm a bit worried about him, that's all."

Sally got out of bed and opened the floor length curtains. The morning sunlight streamed across the grey-green, tile floor.

"Well, maybe he changed his mind. Men do that sometimes, you know."

"It's not like Luther."

"Just go over to Gurney, knock on his door, and

confront him." Sally reached for her robe and towel. "That's what I'd do."

"I know that's what you'd do," Rani replied unhappily. The phone call had stretched her sense of proper boy-girl relations far enough for one day. The idea of walking into the men's dorm was unfathomable. "But, I can't."

"Whatever," her roomie tossed back. "I'm headed for the loo."

Rani dressed in her ankle-length, denim skirt and long-sleeved, polka-dot blouse. She braided her black hair into a thick braid, secured it with a band of plastic flowers, and headed for the dining room. On her way past Gurney Residence Hall, she glanced furtively at Luther's first floor window. The Venetian blinds were drawn tight.

Curled into a ball, Luther Mouana felt wretched. He lay motionless under the heavy wool blanket until his roommate finally left at 8:45. Exhausted and a bit queasy, he carefully sat up and squinted out the window. He stumbled out of bed, rummaged through the top drawer of his dresser until his fingers found the beaded necklace. He kissed the gold cross and pulled it over his head.

Exchanging pjs for boxer shorts and jeans, Luther patted his pocket to be sure his room key was there, grabbed a hooded navy sweatshirt and headed for the exit. Hitting the fire bar with both hands, Luther shoved the metal door open and made a beeline for the Jones Student Center where he bought a Coke and peanut butter crackers in the bookstore before heading for Penington Place as casually as his racing heart would allow.

He stood beside the kitchen porch and studied the foundation stones. There it was: Gideon's secret entrance. Halfway up the second row of stones, the black cast iron door was barely visible behind the shrubbery. Luther slipped between two bushes and crouched down. The thick, green foliage closed behind him, sheltering him from view. He grasped the coiled metal handle and pushed down. He felt the inside bar slide up and out of its latch and jerked the door open to peer into the inky black space where Gideon had spent the past five months. Shaking uncontrollably, he placed both hands on the sill and willed himself to lean forward. His eyes followed the shaft of sunlight to the cement floor, but the blackness refused to surrender any more than a glimpse of the space below. Luther leaned back on his haunches.

"Sweet mother of Jesus," he prayed, "How could Gideon bear to live in a hole blacker than our Somali nights without even a star to comfort or guide him?" Luther's thoughts tumbled over one another. "He said he had a lantern." Luther began to weep. "Oh, Gideon, did you get careless and leave it burning Tuesday night when you were working at the warehouse?"

Luther eased the door closed, made sure it was securely latched, then crawled out between the bushes. Despite a nagging uneasiness, he crossed the campus green with a renewed sense of purpose. When he reached his room, Luther kissed his grandmother's cross.

"Gideon is safe with Professor Hopkins," he said softly. He pulled the beaded necklace over his head and placed it on the handkerchief in the dresser drawer. "That's all that matters right now."

## CHAPTER EIGHTEEN

"Ruthalice, get a load of this." Cliff waved her over to the breakfast nook. "Two artists built a secret apartment in a Rhode Island shopping mall and lived in it for up to three weeks at a time without being detected." He poked the morning paper with his fork. "The artists built a cinderblock wall and nondescript utility door to keep the loft hidden from the outside world."

"No way!" Ruthalice rested her left hand on Cliff's back and read over his shoulder. "'The apartment was fully furnished, including a Sony PlayStation 2 and, since there was no water, they used the mall bathrooms!' What a hoot! A bunch of incredibly unperceptive people must be running that mall for them to get away with something that outlandish!"

"I suspect some poor lowly Pinkerton man is going to lose his job over this." Cliff folded the newspaper. "Listen, honey, this is Friday, so I've got Vet Club at five this afternoon. How 'bout we carpool today and meet at the Leaky Cup around six?"

"Sounds like a plan. We'll decide then what to do about supper."

Like Luther, Richard had also been wide awake at 5:30 a.m. After forty-five minutes of tossing and turning, he got out of bed. "I'm going to the campus," he informed his wife, who waved a sleepy goodbye from under the blankets. Except for the housekeeping staff busily scrubbing and flushing toilets, Richard had Fox

Hall to himself. He picked up the October issue of the *Chronicle of Higher Education* and walked to the window. A red-bellied woodpecker was systematically working its noisy way up the maple tree beside the building.

"Just watching you pounding away makes my head hurt." Richard dropped the *Chronicle* on the coffee table and gazed at the blank computer screen. "I don't even have the energy to water the spider plant," he said wearily. "This is definitely a Leaky Cup morning." He was halfway across Division Street when he realized the coffee shop didn't open for another fifteen minutes. "Phooey," he sputtered. "Oh well, I'll just take a walk around the block."

Twenty minutes later he trotted up the steps under the green sign dangling from the porch soffit: "For Those In The Know, There's No Such Thing As Too Much Joe!" Richard tugged on the front door and checked his watch. Five minutes later the neon lights crackled and a bright red scripted "Open" came to life. Missy Springer opened the door.

"You're bright and early this morning, Richard. You here for a cuppa java?"

He nodded and bent over to stroke the marmalade cat rubbing against his gray slacks. "Biscuit seems to be coping nicely this morning."

"The usual?" Missy asked, turning to the espresso machine.

"I think a tall French vanilla will do the trick this time."

He wrapped both hands around the cup, grateful for the warmth, and made his way back across campus. Maple leaves too weary to hang on any longer decorated the grass still drippy with dew. Here and there a ceiling light came on in one of the dormitories as the campus woke up.

Richard stopped beside his secretary's desk. "You're awfully bright and early this morning," Lynn said cheerfully. A real morning lark, she was always in before the rest of the administrative staff.

"Early, yes; bright, not so much." He tossed his empty cup into the wastebasket. "Vicky and I would like to host the international students for dinner a week from Sunday, say five-thirty. Start with Rani Brown and Luther Mouana, then see how many of the others you can round up to join us." He jerked a handkerchief out of his pants pocket in time to catch three rapid-fire sneezes."

"Bless you."

"Thanks." He wiped his nose and stuffed the hankie back in his pocket. "Notify everyone that I've called a President's Council meeting for three this afternoon. Be sure to include Ruthalice this time," he added through the doorway into his private office. "Oh, keep that ten-thirty slot free, Lynn. I've got to do some work on my remarks for the Penn Place remembrance circle."

That noon a respectable number of faculty, staff, and students stood beside the Reflection Pool and listened as the campus minister and President reflected on the unique history and contribution of Penington Place, the First Sister. "There is only one first," Ruthalice reminded the little gathering. "The first home to the first head of school, the first and only home for the Quaker archives, the first location large enough to host alumni teas, and sadly, the first building on the Emerick College campus to catch fire."

Richard thanked everyone for coming, then walked around Penington Place to check on facilities' progress in securing the building. "Do Not Enter" was spray-painted across the middle of a sheet of plywood barricading the kitchen doorway. "For access, call ext. 600," was printed on a sticky note stuck to the wood.

He called and asked, "Could you send someone over to Penn to let me in?"

Within minutes, the little blue Campus Security cart scooted across the lawn. The guard unlocked the padlock securing the plywood door and wrestled it open. "You don't need to stay," the president said in response to the guard's question. "I'll lock up when I'm finished."

Richard walked across the abandoned kitchen and peered into the murky space below. One-by-eight planks nailed between a pair of two-by-eight support boards created a set of makeshift stairs. Someone had stretched a climbing rope between the kitchen door casing and the fifth support pole at the bottom. Unwilling to trust his safety to the provisional banister alone, Richard pressed the palm of his left hand firmly against the stone wall as he edged his way to the bottom. Having successfully negotiated the descent, he pulled out his cell phone.

"Facilities, this is Judy."

"Judy, Richard Willson here. Tell Angus our top priority is to get a crew down to Penn to clear out the burned furniture, which is where most of the smell of smoke is coming from. Ashes and soot and who knows what else are everywhere down here."

He winced as a rat darted under the charred remains of lounge chairs heaped haphazardly under the staircase. "That's this weekend, Judy. Hire some students and pay overtime if you have to. I want this entire basement cleaned up by Monday morning."

Back upstairs Richard leaned his shoulder into

the makeshift plywood door, secured the padlock, and walked back to his office. He glanced at today's calendar—nothing until the President's Council meeting at three. He sank into the leather desk chair and picked up Chief Turner's report.

The basic facts were straightforward enough. An anonymous 911 call came in at 1:13 a.m. Wednesday morning alerting the police to a fire underway at the college. Richard reviewed a transcript of the exchange between the dispatcher who took the call and Lieutenant Rosemarie Harris, the investigating officer.

"He had kind of a foreign accent."

"The voice was male?"

"Yes."

"What kind of accent?"

"Maybe some kind of African language? The man spoke slowly like he had to think before pronouncing each word." Pause. "His voice was so soft I had to keep asking him to speak up."

He slid the folder to one side and turned to his notes from last night's conversation with the chief. The report was unequivocal: the fire started in the cubbyhole in the wall of the stairwell and spread into the overstuffed furniture piled up under the steps. By the time the fire department arrived at 1:32 a.m., the fire had worked its way up the wooden stairs into the kitchen.

Richard let out a long sigh and closed his eyes. Twenty minutes later Lynn's tap on the door jarred him awake. "It's two-fifty-five, Richard," she said. He gave her a sheepish grin, picked up the file folder and joined his colleagues around the dark oak conference table in what was originally the smallest classroom in Fox Hall. As last one in, Richard pulled the door closed behind him.

"Evelyn and I met with Chief Turner and Lieutenant Harris yesterday afternoon," he nodded his head sideways toward Dean Feller, his eyes meeting those of the other three participants. "Here are the facts as we currently have them."

Ruthalice, tucked between Barbara Carroll, dean of students, and Angus Bailey, director of facilities, wondered why she'd been included this time. Two years ago, President Willson had also summoned the campus minister to the second-floor conference room. Earlier in the day, Matthew Cullen's girlfriend had walked to his apartment to see why he wasn't responding to her texts. She let herself in and discovered him on the floor with a self-inflicted gunshot wound. His death sent the entire campus community into shocked disbelief and grief. The need for her pastoral-care skills had been obvious. A non-fatal fire in the middle of the night where no one even got hurt didn't feel like campus ministry material.

Richard fiddled with his pen before laying it to rest on the table. Evelyn took a sip of water, replaced the cap and set the bottle squarely in the middle of her paper napkin. A collective hush filled the room. Ruthalice Michels was not the only one who sensed a shift in the president's mood. All eyes were focused on the head of the table.

"My friends, that was the easy part." The troubled look on his face drew them all into his concern. "We have a mystery on our collective hands." His gaze settled on the director of facilities, who stirred uncomfortably in his seat. "Angus, I authorized storage of the old parlor furniture four years ago. Considering the events of the past few days, this may not have been one of my better decisions, but that's all water under the bridge at this point I'm afraid."

Evelyn took up the narrative.

"There were fireworks in Hannah Emerick's storage compartment, hidden behind wads of crumpled up newspaper and cardboard boxes."

Ruthalice felt her stomach tighten. *I don't like the direction this is going one little bit.* Next to her Barbara Carroll covered her mouth and coughed into the palm of her hand.

Angus swiveled his chair back and forth repeatedly bumping its arms against the table. "I don't see how that can happen," he said. "Penington is locked up tight as a drum the minute Ernestine goes home,"

"I want to know why anyone would stash explosives in Penn in the first place."

"To blow it up"

"Oh, come on, Angus," Evelyn responded sharply, "Surely you don't believe that. Next you'll be telling us this is a student protest gone awry."

"I said no such thing," Angus shot back.

The academic dean and the director of facilities seldom saw eye to eye on anything from the color to paint the women's bathrooms to the fundamental nature of humankind.

"OK, that's enough speculation." The bickering ceased immediately. "Permit me to read from my personal notes of last evening's conversation with Chief Turner and Lieutenant Harris." The president eyeballed each of his colleagues in turn over the top of his glasses. "All evidence indicates that the newspaper in the recess ignited first. Fire subsequently spread to the box of fireworks, which exploded, spewing burning material out over the open staircase, igniting the furniture below."

*You call someone who starts fires on purpose an arsonist.*
Ruthalice shivered. *Rani's mysterious hooded figure; boasting about a spectacular fire.* Her forehead began to pound. *My God, what's going on?*

"Richard, that's all very well and good as far as it goes, but we have no explanation for how the newspapers caught fire." Angus crossed his arms and surveyed his colleagues. "Am I right?"

Richard ignored him.

"Turner promised the complete report will be on my desk first thing Monday morning. If this turns out to be an in-house issue, we will deal with it through the college judicial system, unless, of course, it has wider implications. In the meantime, if you must speculate, do so only amongst yourselves. Everyone clear on that?"

Heads nodded in unison around the table.

"I'd like to summarize things a bit if I could," Ruthalice spoke into the awkward silence. "Someone went to a great deal of effort to disguise the fact they put fireworks in the cubbyhole. So, my first question is, who goes into the basement of Penn these days?"

"Our arsonist did, unless we have a case of spontaneous combustion," Angus retorted.

"Ruthalice's question is a good one." Barbara adjusted her gold necklace, so it lay flat across her throat. "I think Ernestine Perkins is the logical person to ask about access. She runs a tight ship over there."

"Let me make a phone call." The president rose and disappeared into the hallway. The little group occupied itself drinking from water bottles and gazing out the window.

*Firecrackers are gorgeous and loud; they call attention to themselves and can be seen all over town!* Ruthalice ran her sweaty palms the length of her thighs.

"What are you pondering over there, Ruthalice?" Barbara gently nudged her. "Your eyebrows are bobbing up and down like corks."

Ruthalice blushed.

"I'm trying to figure out who wanted fireworks on campus and why, that's all."

"When you get that one figured out, be sure to share it with the rest of us."

"I will be sure to do that, Angus," she replied, returning his sullen stare with a bright smile.

"Ernestine Perkins assures me no one from her office has been in the basement since the second of June," Richard announced, as he settled back into his chair. "She needed records for an article she was writing about the class of 1876." He paused, a pensive look crossing his face. "That was Emerick's first graduating class with its seven students."

"But those records are in the Quaker Archives," Ruthalice protested, remembering her promise to write a short history for the new brochure being prepared for Parents Weekend. "I know because I asked for them myself just last week."

"Well Ernestine must have forgotten that because she sent her student worker to the basement."

"So, what does this intriguing piece of information tell us?" Angus grumbled.

"That as far as our director of alumni relations is concerned, no one's been in the basement in four months." Evelyn scratched above her left ear with her index finger. "Which would indicate that whoever it was either has a key to the building or was in the basement during office hours, unbeknownst to Ernestine."

"The latter is more likely, I should think," the dean of students offered. "Penn's accessible every weekday during the day. It'd be pretty easy to slip in undetected."

Richard cleared his throat.

"There's more." The room fell silent. "I got my coffee at the Leaky Cup this morning. Missy Springer told me she saw a couple of college-aged people hanging around between Penington and the meetinghouse around twelve-thirty Wednesday morning. I urged her to inform Chief Turner, which I'm sure she has done by now."

Richard finished the bottle of warm water in front of him before continuing.

"Lynn told me that while I was on the phone with Ernestine, Chief Turner called to inform us he's issued a request for anyone with information about two young men seen loitering around the southwest end of campus Wednesday morning to contact the witness hotline at the Oakes Quarry Police Department or the Boone County Sheriff's office. Quote, a reward is offered for information which leads to the arrest and conviction of the party or parties involved in Wednesday's fire at Emerick College, unquote."

"Did Missy say 'men' or 'people'?"

"Oh, for heaven's sakes, Ruthalice, do we have to be politically correct twenty-four seven?" Angus shook his head. "What difference does it make?"

Richard rose wearily to his feet.

"OK folks, now you know as much as I do," he said, staying out of the long-running feud over inclusive language. "Let's all go home and sleep on it. Give me a buzz if the bright bulb of insight lights up in the middle of the night, OK?" His steady smile belied his uneasiness. "And remember, your conjectures are welcome in my office and nowhere else."

As the council members filed out, the president lightly touched Ruthalice's arm.

"Ruthalice, may I have a word, and with you also, Babs?"

He quietly closed the door.

"Ruthalice, I need you to keep your ear to the ground, to coin a rather corny phrase. The students trust you, and you're often told things in confidence." He paused looking slightly uncomfortable. "I'm well aware of the confidentiality of the confessional, so to speak, but I'm requesting that you report anything you hear immediately and directly to me whether it seems pertinent or not."

Turning to the dean of students he added, "Babs, I'm asking the same of you. "

"I'll call my RAs together this evening," she replied without hesitation, "and see what the rumors are in the resident halls. Our students often hear things they don't want to pass along to me."

"Well someone on this campus knows who, why, and probably how. The president of our Board of Trustees is worried that if this does turn out to be arson, the insurance adjustor may try to finagle out of as much coverage as possible."

Ruthalice suddenly felt miserable. "I dread the thought of where we could end up with that line of investigation."

The president nodded his head. "I just want this figured out in a timely manner, so we can get on with the business of higher education."

Ruthalice waited until Evelyn reached the staircase. "Let's go down to your office, Richard," she said. "One of our international students shared a conversation she overheard in the bathroom. I think you should know about it."

Twenty minutes later, Richard opened the office door and reached for his coat. "You and Clifford have a good weekend," he said.

"Isn't this the weekend your sister visits?" Ruthalice replied, waiting while he turned out the lights.

"Yes," he said smiling. "It will be good to see her in spite of all the brouhaha on campus."

# CHAPTER NINETEEN

C liff returned to his office at four-fifteen, nudged the partially open door with his elbow and nearly collided with Charles Hopkins pacing impatiently between door and window.

"My goodness, Charles. It's the middle of the afternoon. What brings you to my humble abode?"

"I'm hoping you and Ruthalice are free for dinner tonight." Before Cliff could answer, he hurried on, "I'd be dreadfully appreciative if you could join me at the house round seven. I find myself in a bit of a muddle. I could use your collective discernment."

"Sounds positively intriguing."

"Then that settles it. I'll see you both tonight."

Cliff dutifully left a message for the campus minister on her answering machine, then sat down determined to grade at least five student lab books before it was time to meet with the Vets of Tomorrow Club.

For his part, Charles decided to take a walk and mull over the evening's event with the M&Ms. It was one of those cloudless blue sky, gorgeous crisp air, Friday afternoons only a midwestern fall can produce. He walked briskly across the city park and sat on a warped wooden bench beside the deserted picnic shelter. A motley handful of white farm ducks waddled around the pond comingling with a half-dozen mallards. Charles closed his eyes and let the turmoil of the past twenty-four hours parade across his mind.

It had been two o'clock in the morning before he finally bid his Somali guests good night and tumbled fully clothed into bed for the second night in a row. When he shuffled into the kitchen at eight and found no trace of either Luther or Gideon, Charles began to fret. Too many secrets were piling up; there was too much coming and going to watch over and contain. But most terrifying of all was the image of his nosey next-door neighbor popping around uninvited for a look-see if she got even the slightest whiff of a rumor that Professor Charles E. Hopkins was harboring an undocumented alien. He could see it all unfolding with appalling predictability. The thought that an African male, no doubt a Muslim, was living on Sheppard Place with its law-abiding citizens would send Laverna Stroodle into a tizzy. It would be out of a sense of patriotic fervor that Stroodle would turn her neighbor of more than thirty years over to the proper authorities.

Two of the ducks got into a scuffle over a piece of stale bread that one of them discovered a few feet from Charles' bench. "It's definitely not worth fighting over," he reminded them as he got to his feet. He walked back to the Edward Hicks Fine Arts Building parking lot and persuaded his ornery VW Beetle to carry him home one more time.

As he entered the empty kitchen, the soft strains of Beethoven's Pastoral Symphony greeted him from the living room. "There's never been someone to come home to before," he grumbled, uncertain whether he liked the idea or not. For an instant he resented the fact his domicile had been invaded. He brushed the feeling aside and headed to the refrigerator to start preparing dinner for his guests.

A short while later the music ended, and he looked up at an unexpected sound in the ensuing silence. "Oh, hello Gideon. I didn't hear you come in. I have a little surprise for you," he added, wiping his hands on a faded dish towel. "Our campus minister and her biology professor husband are joining us for dinner this evening." A momentary look of panic darted across Gideon's face. "Ruthalice and Clifford are colleagues of mine. We've been friends for years and years." Charles tossed the potatoes in a pot of water. "The truth is, Gideon, your situation with me is precarious. Ruthalice and Clifford are people we can trust to help keep you safe."

"You are in trouble, Professor Curly, because of me," Gideon said dejectedly. "I should not be here." His eyes darted toward the basement door. "I go now."

"Whoa, whoa!" Charles reached out and grabbed the young man by both shoulders. "You're not going anywhere." He loosened his grip and took a step back, surveying the young man from head to toe. "I want you to stay here with me, but I can't do this alone. My friends are kind, generous, sensible people who will be delighted to meet you."

Gideon raised his head. "Can Luther join us also?"

Charles reached for the white plastic wall phone and waited for the answering machine to pick up. "Luther, this is Professor Hopkins. Gideon and I would like to talk with you again, so please come to my house when you get this message."

"Thank you, Professor Curly." He backed into the hallway. "Now I get clean shirt and help you set the table for our guests."

"Excellent. I'm headed for a quick shower. Be a sport would you and turn on that outside light. The switch is on the wall by the front door."

While the professor took a shower, Gideon went straight to his basement room and changed his shirt, then headed back upstairs, eager to show Professor

Curly he knew how to set the table for dinner. He paused at the top of the stairs.

"Jesus, you lay right upon my heart. Please to give me courage and peace. I am very nervous." Gideon lifted the crucifix to his lips. "I trust Professor Curly." He hesitated. "And his friends."

Gideon opened drawers until he located the silverware, took four of everything and began placing knives, forks, and spoons around the kitchen table. "I put knife on right and fork on left," he reminded himself at each placemat. Humming happily, Gideon added plates and glasses, then stood back to admire his handiwork.

"Jolly good, old boy. Not bad for a bloke who's been camping out in the basement for five months." He thumped the young man on the back. "But the spoon goes over here." He glanced up at the wall clock. "It's too soon to start the veggie water. Let's go through to the front room. I could use a drink."

Gideon assumed his place on the loveseat whose English hunting scene upholstery had seen better days and laid his right arm on the herringbone throw pillow. Charles sank into his favorite armchair and uncorked the sherry.

"Gracious, we're becoming damnably predictable in our habits, Gideon. Like a couple old duffers taking their self-designated seats in a gentleman's club." The professor raised his glass. "Well, cheers! Don't you want something to drink whilst we wait? A Coke or lemonade?"

"I get a Coke."

Gideon disappeared into the kitchen, then resumed his position on the sofa. He set the can on the carpet, rested his palms on his legs and stared at the picture on the opposite wall. Charles watched as Gideon studied his hands, then slid them back and forth on his trousers. His nervousness became apparent as an involuntary shiver caused him to rigorously rub the tip of his nose with the heel of his left hand.

"You're worried about my colleagues and wonder if you can trust them. Am I correct?" Charles asked, sipping his sherry.

"What do I tell them, Professor Curly?"

"The truth. That is what we are both going to do, my young friend. Speak the truth."

# CHAPTER TWENTY

As the doorbell rang, Charles set his drink on the side table, then got to his feet. "Do not fret, my young friend, I will get us started."

Gideon took a deep breath and pressed his back deep into the cushion. At the sound of strange voices, the familiar cramps seized his intestines.

"Sweet Mary, mother of Jesus, help me," he implored, rising quickly to his feet and slipping between the loveseat and the harpsichord. He squeezed his eyes and began to pray. "Do not let them send me back, please, no! I rather hide away in America than die in Somalia."

"Gideon, I want you to meet my colleagues, Ruthalice Michels and Clifford Mowry." Sweeping his arm toward the young man, Charles added in his booming voice, "Ruthalice, Cliff, meet my young Somali friend, Gideon Boseka."

At the sound of his name, Gideon opened his eyes.

"How nice to meet you, Gideon." Ruthalice smiled warmly and stepped forward extending her hand. Seeing his hesitancy, she stopped moving. "I taught at the Friends Theological College in Kaimosi, Kenya, for six months." She paused, lowering her arm. "We had one student, Salome Kutosi, whose mother lives in Mogadishu."

The two men held their collective breath as Gideon, his left hand in the crook of his right arm, tentatively offered his hand. As their hands met, the heavy cloak of tension seemed to slip off the young man's shoulders and tumble to the floor.

"I am from Doolow on the Jubba River. I am a Christian," he added hastily, "not a Muslim."

"I know, Gideon," Ruthalice replied softly. "That is a lovely beaded necklace."

His hand flew instinctively to his throat.

"Oh, yes. I wear the necklace my grandmother makes for me." His face relaxed into a charming smile. "It is Grandmother who named me Gideon."

"The faithful judge of the Israelites whom the Lord chose to lead his people out of oppression by the hand of Midian." Ruthalice turned to Cliff. "My husband teaches biology here at Emerick College."

Clifford shook Gideon's hand, then stepped back and crossed his arms, a warm twinkle lighting his brown eyes.

"If I remember my geography correctly, Doolow is located on the northern border of Somalia near Ethiopia and Kenya where the three borders come together."

"Yes, yes! My people raise cattle. Because cattle bring wealth and status, many herders are hurt or killed in the fighting over grazing and water." He sighed. "My country is too dry."

Cliff nodded and scratched his chin.

"Gideon, have we met somewhere before? You look vaguely familiar."

"Dear me, look at us standing like stumps in the doorway." Their host closed the front door and shoved Cliff into the room. "I'm not being much of a host. Do sit down and I'll get us a drink. Sherry or port?"

"My goodness, Charles," Ruthalice exclaimed from her seat on the sofa. "Something smells simply delicious. Can I be of assistance?"

"Not quite yet, my dear. All that remains is to put veggies in boiling water and warm the muffins."

Content for the moment with their pre-dinner small talk, Cliff sipped his sherry and agreed that the Cincinnati Bengals were off to another lousy start. Curly decided that Cliff was safely diverted from his trip down memory lane and accepted Ruthalice's offer of help. The two of them disappeared into the kitchen chatting happily about the upcoming Oakes Quarry Nature Club color tour on Sunday.

Left unattended, Clifford tried again.

"I pride myself on never forgetting a face. It's one of my little quirks, I guess."

Gideon looked confused and was about to speak when their host reappeared.

"Dinner is ready now. Please come through."

A confirmed bachelor, Charles Hopkins saw no need for a big house. Content with his two-bedroom bungalow, he entertained the occasional dinner guest at the one-leaf oval table in the middle of his modest kitchen.

"Love the color scheme, Charles," Ruthalice said apropos of nothing during an awkward silence as the serving dishes were passed.

"Wheat walls with daffodil trim," he said. "I was told these colors would make the kitchen warm and welcoming." An alarming shade of red crept up his neck.

"Good heavens, Charles, you didn't hire an interior decorator." Cliff leaned back in his chair and grinned.

"Mrs. Stroodle and her damnable poodle." He let out a heavy sigh. "From next door."

Ruthalice burst out laughing. "Oh, Charles, you can't be serious. Oh no," she said, looking at his face,

"You are serious."

"Let me just say I no longer find her amusing." He glared out the kitchen window. "In fact, she has the potential to become a frightful nuisance."

"I've got it!" Cliff slapped his palm on the table. "I told you I never forgot a face." He beamed at Gideon across the table. "You were in my human biology course six or seven years ago. Yes, I'm sure of it."

Gideon froze. Charles' fork stopped halfway to his mouth. Nodding vigorously, Cliff plowed ahead.

"You turned in some of the most professional looking lab reports I've ever received from a student. And your drawings!" Cliff's voice trailed off as he became aware of the silence engulfing the room.

Ruthalice gently took Cliff's hand. Charles finished putting the fork in his mouth and began to chew. Gideon remained motionless, staring at something only he could see. Then, into the hush, Gideon began to speak.

"You are right, Professor Clifford," he said, his coal-black eyes staring self-consciously across the table. "I was a student at Emerick College." Gideon's smile, always just beneath the surface, burst across his face. "Thank you for the compliment, Professor Clifford. I work very, very hard on my laboratory report notebook." Looking at his hands he added, "I like to draw."

Cliff leaned back in his chair. "So I was right after all."

"You never forget a face," Gideon repeated. His smile was pensive. "I like Emerick College very much. It was good time for me."

"Well, we got through that," Charles announced getting to his feet. He turned on the coffee pot and began to scoop prodigious amounts of Neapolitan ice cream into four mismatched, earthenware bowls. Cliff

pushed back and started to clear the table. Gideon produced a box of Chips Ahoy chocolate chip cookies from
the shelf above the toaster. A series of short taps interrupted the comfortable domestic scene. Ruthalice
glimpsed a face peeking through the kitchen door window.

"It's Luther," Charles reminded Gideon, who
looked about to bolt. "Remember, we invited him to
join us tonight."

As his young compatriot stepped into the room,
Gideon fell into the other man's arms as they embraced.

"You're just in time for dessert." Charles waved his
hand in the air indicating the rest of the table. "You
probably already know these folks, Luther, Ruthalice
Michels, our campus minister, and Clifford Mowry, professor of biology."

Luther acknowledged them with a low bow from
the waist.

"I am taking the invertebrate zoology class this semester from Clifford," he said. "I'm studying to be a
large animal veterinarian. I'm going to return home and
teach our Somali herdsmen how to provide better care
to our cattle."

Luther stuffed his hands into the pockets of his ny-
lon windbreaker. "And I have seen you on campus, Pastor Ruthalice."

"Put those biscuits on a plate," Charles said, looking at Gideon. "Let's go through to the front room, and
I'll bring the dessert tray. We have much to discuss this
evening."

Clifford headed for the second armchair, Ruthalice
chose the loveseat, and Luther perched on the edge of
the harpsichord bench.

"Oh, no, Luther, that seat is dreadfully uncomfortable. Clifford, be a good sport and fetch that chair with the padded seat. It's in my study." Charles set the battered silver tray on the table between the two armchairs. "Who needs cream and sugar? I've also brewed tea for us English sorts who can't abide coffee more than once a day."

"I like black coffee at night," Luther replied. "It keeps me awake so I can pull the all-nighters."

Cliff returned and placed the chair with the padded seat beside the small sofa, picked up the remaining ice cream bowl, and sat down.

"So Luther, what brings you here this evening, other than the fact that Professor Hopkins summoned you?"

Luther and Gideon exchanged a nearly imperceptible glance.

"I thought the two boys might have something in common," Charles began, then added, "since they're both from Somalia."

"So Gideon," Cliff said, "do you and Luther have something in common?"

Ruthalice turned to Gideon who had settled in beside her on the loveseat. "Gideon, I have known Charles Hopkins for over four years now. He and Clifford and I have shared many, many secrets during that time."

She smiled at the two professors across the room. Clifford licked his ice cream spoon and waited. From the corner of her eye Ruthalice saw Luther softly touch Gideon's knee with his left hand. "Whatever you share with us tonight," she continued gently, "remains in this room."

"Gideon," Charles said with gentle resolve, "it is time to tell the truth. Luther Mouana and Gideon Boseka are cousins." Gideon's lips moving silently as he began to pray under his breath.

"That is correct," Luther stated plainly. "My mother is Gideon's mother's youngest cousin." He turned to Ruthalice. "My mother has ten older sisters and two younger brothers." Grinning broadly, he added, "My grandfather was very pleased to finally get his grandsons."

Ruthalice glanced at Cliff, who sat with his legs crossed. His pensive gaze moved from Gideon to Luther and back again.

"I'm still a bit puzzled here, guys," Cliff said casually. "You graduated in, what was it, Gideon, 2000, and you Luther came to Emerick in 2004. Since you're taking Invertebrate this fall, you must be a junior, which means you two did not overlap." He ran a quick mental check to be sure his math was accurate. "What's the name of your hometown?"

"Chisimaio," Luther replied quickly, "on the southern coast of Somalia." He paused. "Because the port is so deep, Chisimaio is one of Somalia's most important commercial centers. My father works at the docks offloading enormous ocean liners steaming in and out of the Indian Ocean."

Ruthalice shifted in her seat. *What about the pirates?* She was about to ask when Luther deftly passed the conversation baton to his cousin.

"Professor Clifford is right again." Gideon unfolded and sat up straight on the sofa. "I graduate in 2000. Then I find a job in Cleveland and work in hospital laboratory. That is where I meet my wife, Serita."

Dropping his head, Gideon squeezed the corners of his eyes with thumb and forefinger. Charles took up the story.

"Serita was an American citizen of Ethiopian descent. She and Gideon were married for two years." He cleared his throat. "Serita and their baby girl died in childbirth."

The steady tick-tock of the grandfather clock measured out the silence.

"I already started my application for citizenship, but when my wife died, ICE government agent come and tell me I will be deported." Gideon seemed to wilt. "Nobody trust a young, single Somali man in America anymore."

"Nine-eleven." Charles declared. His angry gaze landed briefly on each one of them. "Our young friend here is one of the numerous nameless and uncounted victims of this government's response to that terrorist attack."

"Yes, nine-one-one," Gideon chose each word carefully. "I am not a Muslim man, but Immigration does not care. I am alone and black and from Somalia—a Muslim country with much poverty, violence, and killings. We are declared US enemy."

Gideon fingered the crucifix around his neck and raised his eyes.

"I tell them I cannot go back. There is no home for me. My house is destroyed in the fighting. My mother and my father and my little sister are all killed. I am a refugee in my country too." He gulped, his eyes filling with tears. "I beg to finish my citizenship papers so I can keep my job at the hospital. Then I can go to graduate school in Ohio, but ICE man tell me, how you say? 'no go.' You cannot stay."

Gideon pressed his slender body into the corner of the loveseat, a look of utter despair on his face. "So I disappear from Cleveland and hospital job. I ran to my mentor." Gideon shrugged as if to say, what else could I do? "Dr. Martin find me a safe place to hide—he calls it my sanctuary."

"His sanctuary, as dear old TM labelled it, is right here." Charles pointed at the floor. "Gideon has been living in the coal bin in the basement of Penington Place." He picked up the heavy glass decanter and poured himself a third glass of sherry. "Refill anyone?"

Cliff held out his glass; Luther declined with a shake of his head. Gideon stared at his lap.

"Charles, that can't be true," Ruthalice cried, but one look at Gideon told her otherwise. She waved off a refill. "So, then, who is this Dr. Martin? And is this the same person as 'TM'?"

"I can help you here, Sweetheart. Dr. Terrell Martin was the Romance Languages professor at Emerick in the late fifties, early sixties." Cliff looked at Charles for confirmation. "Professor Martin had been retired for years by the time you came here as a student, Gideon." Cliff looked puzzled. "If memory serves, he only came to campus when someone expressly invited him."

"I did not meet Professor Martin at Emerick College. We meet in Mogadishu."

"Terrell Martin had recently retired from college teaching and was engaged in humanitarian work for the United Nations in Somalia," Charles explained. "He was stationed in Mogadishu and met Gideon one afternoon in the mission's charity soup line. They both spoke enough Arabic to communicate, and by evening, Martin had it in his head that this lad needed to go to college, and Emerick was the right place. He and our friend here spent a good many hours together, as it turns out. So in typical take-charge fashion, he set about making it happen." Charles held his sherry glass up. "Old Professor Martin took quite a shine to you, Gideon."

Gideon beamed. "Dr. Martin said, 'You are very bright, Gideon, and will make an excellent student. Emerick College will be proud of you.'"

"OK, now wait a minute. Can we back up? I'm confused." Ruthalice raised both hands as if to ward off any more surprises. "Gideon's been right here on campus, under our very noses, for how long?"

"Five months," Charles said flatly. "Gideon Boseka returned to Oakes Quarry in the middle of May."

"And you never said one word to anybody?" Ruthalice took a deep breath, struggling to keep the distress she felt out of her voice.

"However," he added, holding up his hand in self-defense, "I didn't know Gideon was here until six weeks ago."

"When I get in trouble with Immigration in Cleveland, I call Dr. Martin," Gideon said, his voice devoid of emotion. "He said come to Oakes Quarry and I will take care of you. So I stay with him until one night, Dr. Martin wakes me up. 'ICE is coming, Gideon. You are not safe here with me anymore. You must hide in the basement of Penington Place where you will be safe.'"

Gideon jumped as a car door slammed somewhere down the block. "Dr. Martin is almost correct. No one comes down to basement very much, and when the girl comes, I hear her steps and stay quiet. She never knows I am there." His voice trailed off. "In Somalia, I stay quiet, and I survive the soldier raids on my village."

"I find this utterly amazing," Cliff said, leaning forward. "How on earth were you able to get in and out of the basement undetected?"

"Dr. Martin show me a little metal door behind the bushes."

"Of course," Ruthalice exclaimed, "the coal bin door on the south side. Thank you, Biscuit."

Seeing the quizzical looks all around her, Ruthalice quickly explained, "I was poking around Penn Place Wednesday afternoon looking for I'm not exactly sure what, when Missy Springer's cat came out of the bushes, and I caught a glimpse of a metal door handle. We had a coal bin in the house where I grew up, so it didn't strike me as anything unusual or significant." An involuntary shiver slid up her spine. "I don't know how on earth you managed, Gideon. It's gotta be pitch black down there and damp and oh, I don't know," she shuddered, "creepy!"

"Dr. Martin give me oil lantern," he replied, "and a blanket. I have my clothes and some books." Seeing the look of horror on her face, Gideon added reassuringly. "It's OK to live in Penington Place, Miss Ruthalice. I go out at night and sleep in daytime."

Charles picked up the narrative. "Our friend here timed his nightly comings and goings with the routine of the Alumni Office workers and the security man who, I might note, patrols in a frightfully predictable pattern every weeknight. So Gideon remained totally undetected."

"They built a nondescript utility door to keep their loft hidden from the mall shoppers," Ruthalice murmured under her breath.

"Say what?" Charles looked lost.

"Ruthalice's just recalling an AP story from the *Dayton Daily News* she found unbelievable at the time." Cliff grinned. "I believe 'no way!' was her analytical response to the ostensible episode."

"Ah, quite." Charles set his sherry glass on the table. "I thought the same thing when I read that story." He winked playfully at Ruthalice.

Unable to follow their banter, Gideon studied his cousin's face. He was certain that, despite his placid face and unfurrowed brow, Luther's mind was filling with unanswerable questions. Only his fellow countryman could truly understand the need to remain hidden. The cousins had witnessed unspeakable times of torture, rape, and murder as Somalia deteriorated and sank into a violence, which no one seemed able or willing to control. *If they catch you, my son, they will kill you.*

Gideon forced himself back to the present and the temporary safety of Professor Curly's dimly lit living room.

"I eat what Professor Martin bring me sometimes, and sometimes I go to dumpster behind Jones Center. I always have something to eat. Finally, I apply for job." Gideon glanced over his shoulder at the closed curtains behind him. "I sweep the storeroom. Then stock boy quit, so now I restock shelves. A big promotion," he added, pleased with himself. "If warehouse is clean and shelves full when boss lady comes at 4 a.m., I keep good job."

Luther joined the story telling.

"We Somalis have learned how to live on very little. We live what you Quakers call the simple life." He grinned. "And now, my cousin, you are saving money to join our aunts and uncles in Minneapolis-St. Paul someday."

"Twin Cities." The two men chuckled at some shared family memory. Then a cloud seemed to pass over Gideon's face.

"I was safe for five months. Now I am fugitive again.

I must run and hide." Gideon's face filled with sadness. "This time, Papa," he whispered, "I never look back."

Ruthalice bit her lip, certain she would burst into tears if she so much as glanced at the young man seated beside her on the loveseat. Cliff studied the bottom of his empty glass, pondering the unfairness of it all. Recalling his own childhood terror every time the air raid sirens sent him into the unlit tunnels under the streets of London, Charles wondered how his young Somali friend kept his sanity. Luther studied his cousin thinking of him now as "born-again Gideon" and wondered what life might be like for the two of them to be together. If he stayed in Oakes Quarry, there would finally be someone he could share the terrible fear that often came with the setting of the sun.

Gideon's calm voice broke into the heavy silence. "The coal bin was my home." He smiled his gentle smile. "It is very quiet. I like quiet." The cousins exchanged another private glance.

Clifford rested his elbows on his knees. He intertwined his fingers and gazed intently at Gideon.

"Didn't anyone ever stop and question you?" Always the practical one, Clifford unwittingly moved the conversation into a place less fraught with emotion.

"One morning on way back from my job, a policewoman stops me in the parking lot. She ask me where I am going and I say, 'to the college', and she ask me where I live and I say, 'at the college', and she say 'Good night.' So, you see," he said, grinning contentedly, "I not lie; I tell the truth."

"And that was that?" Ruthalice managed to ask.

"I go home, and she walk away." Gideon laughed and clapped his hands. "That was that!"

Their host got to his feet and, without a word, disappeared into the kitchen. He re-emerged five minutes later bearing a second round of coffee, hot tea, and cookies. Cliff stretched his legs in front of him, stuffed both hands into his jacket pockets, and gave an enormous yawn. Ruthalice rolled her shoulders to relieve the tension, raised both arms above her head and swallowed—*my heart back into my chest*—and turned to Luther.

"So, tell me. Did you know your cousin was living on campus?"

Luther shook his head. "We knew nothing of each other's whereabouts until last night when Professor Hopkins forced me to come to his house." Luther burst out laughing and pointed his index finger at the old professor, who chuckled appreciatively.

"Our family is very large," Gideon said. "My cousin and I were separated by civil war when we were young children. We never see each other again until last night in this house."

Ruthalice took Gideon's right hand, then reached across the space between them and gently clasped Luther's left one in hers.

"Loving and ever-present God," she prayed in a firm voice. "We are filled with thanksgiving for your mercy, and we thank you from the depths of our being for reuniting these two, precious people. I ask a special blessing for our dear Charles who made it possible."

She released their hands and fumbled in her skirt pocket for a tissue. She blew her nose, then dropped the damp Kleenex in the wastebasket beside the sofa.

"I see that each of you is wearing the beaded necklace made by your grandmother. It is your talisman?"

"Our birthmark," Luther said smiling with pleasure. "It is how we recognized each other."

As the cookies made the rounds, the mood lightened. Voices rose and fell as parents walked by outside returning home from the high school football game. A high-pitched yipping suddenly began in the yard next door.

"Ah," said Charles. "The insufferable poodle of Mrs. Stroodle, out for his nightly doggy constitutional."

Ruthalice nearly choked on her cookie. The barking grew louder, then ceased as abruptly as it had begun.

"I had a dog once," Gideon said in that third-person announcer voice he often used when speaking about his childhood. "One day Buddy disappeared. We find out a neighbor man eat him because he is very hungry. My mother says we believe him."

Luther nodded. "All over Somalia people are starving."

"But here in Ohio is OK. I have job and nice boss lady who come in at four in morning and never ask me questions."

# CHAPTER TWENTY-ONE

The M&Ms stood on the front stoop and, promising to get together again soon, headed for home. The cul-de-sac was deserted, lit only by tall streetlamps and the occasional porchlight. The curved slice of moon had begun its ascent across the star-strewn sky above Oakes Quarry.

"I'm still a bit stunned by Charles' complete involvement in this whole saga," Cliff said, braking for a white cat that suddenly shot out between two parked cars, "though now that I think about it, I guess I really shouldn't be. Charles was just a kid himself during the air raids on London and was forced to hide for hours in the Goodge Street Underground Station. He doesn't talk about it much, but the terror of those endless, unbearable nights must be just below the surface. I suspect he has immense empathy for a homeless orphan and war refugee like himself."

As they reached the edge of town, Cliff clicked on the high beams and settled into a comfortable fifty miles per hour. Reaching for Ruthalice's hand, he interlaced their fingers and squeezed gently.

"Tell me, Sweetheart. What doth my dear campus minister have to say?"

"I don't know what to think, Cliff. I'm still marveling at Gideon's ability to remain undetected on our little campus for over five months when everyone seems to know what everyone else has said and done within minutes. Hidden in plain sight."

Ruthalice gazed out the passenger window. Orion the Hunter, his belt of three stars shining at his waist, stood poised to shoot his arrow across the coal black sky. An enormous inflated Halloween pumpkin, its insides aglow with artificial light, bobbed and wobbled in the front yard of Sky View Farms.

"Consumerism run amok," she observed cryptically.

"Hmmm?"

"Oh, nothing. I'm just a bit cranky that's all." She continued to stare out the window. "After listening to Gideon talk about subsisting on handouts and leftovers, and Luther reminiscing about hundreds of thousands of people starving in Somali, I'm not in the mood for over-blown Halloween decorations, that's all."

"Gideon indicated that his boss lady at the warehouse is sympathetic to his plight because her brother's an illegal alien."

Ruthalice slipped her hand out of his and laid her palm against the back of Cliff's neck, gently fingering his curly hair.

"Undocumented is the proper term these days, Cliff, undocumented worker." Sensing his annoyance, she added quickly, "I actually prefer that language because according to Scripture, we are all aliens living on a land that belongs to the Lord. So, biblically speaking, there is no such thing as an illegal alien." Ruthalice ran her thumb along Clifford's cheek tracing the line of his jaw. "I don't think God spends a whole lot of time worrying about national boundaries. And besides, it's another reminder to the pastor side of me that all six billion of us are one big human family. We may not get along very well, but we do have an awful lot in common."

"Her brother is undocumented." Cliff landed heavily on the last word. "At any rate, the fact that his boss lady assured him no one would ask any questions if he just laid low and did his job, turned out to be correct. She and Charles were the only ones who knew Gideon was in town." Cliff slowed down and pulled off on the right-hand shoulder as an ambulance appeared in the rearview mirror.

"Terrell Martin knew."

"Correct, but he had a stroke and his daughter, Dorothy, insisted he come live with her, so Martin moved up to Toledo. I should think that put him out of the picture for all intents and purposes. Also, remember that after Martin moved to Toledo, Gideon only heard from him once when he sent a letter via Charles to let Gideon know he'd been 'kidnapped,' as he put it, by his youngest child."

"OK, let me be sure I've got this straight: five months ago, Terrell Martin is the only person who knows Gideon Boseka is back on campus. Then, when he moved up to Toledo in August, Martin passed Gideon on to Charles to look after." Ruthalice pulled her coat around her shoulders. "I'm guessing Immigration has lost track of his whereabouts by now."

"Is that wishful thinking?"

"Probably," Ruthalice replied with a sigh.

Cliff stopped at the mailbox and extracted a rubber-banded bundle of Christmas catalogs.

"I suspect when Gideon disappeared from Cleveland, Charles didn't know any more than anyone else did about his whereabouts because for some reason Terrell Martin wasn't ready to spill the beans." He laid the mail in Ruthalice's lap. "Once he got a job, a boss lady to cover for him, and a friend on campus to provide occasional comfort, Gideon settled into the cellar of Penington Place."

"It's incredible to me how people manage to live between the proverbial rock and a hard place when all the choices are fraught with danger."

"Like the hermit crab who scurries defenselessly from one shell to another, staying put until the shelter no longer fits."

The garage door went up, allowing them to pass through, then landed with a thud on the cement floor behind them. Ruthalice retrieved her purse from the back seat and opened the car door.

"It's impossible to walk even a block in Gideon's shoes, let alone a whole mile. Just thinking about living all by myself with no one to come home to makes me want to weep." She stared at the cinder-block wall. "Gideon hasn't even had sufficient time to mourn the death of his wife and baby daughter."

Ruthalice gathered up the mail Cliff had tossed in her lap.

"He's clinging to a precarious present, escaping an unbearable past, and facing a future of what? endless hiding and running? What good does his hard-earned Emerick College degree do him when he's forced to live a furtive, secret existence underground, popping in and out like a gopher spooked by his own shadow?" she asked, climbing out of the front seat.

Cliff slipped around the front of the car and gathered his wife into his strong, loving arms. Still clinging to her, he opened the kitchen door. They stood in the dark mudroom, lost in their own private thoughts. Finally, Ruthalice stepped into the kitchen, set the catalogs and purse on the kitchen counter, and filled the teakettle with water.

"I can't possibly get to sleep yet, Cliff. I'm too wound up." She lifted two mugs off their hooks under the kitchen cabinet. "Will you join me for Chocolate Raspberry Delight cocoa?"

"Sure. If we're going to be up for a while, what do you say to a little fire?"

Cliff headed for the living room without waiting for a reply. By the time Ruthalice slipped off her shoes, heat from the fire had reached the green leather couch.

"You know what I want to do, Cliff? I want to move Gideon out here in the country, declare Horsefeathers Farm a sanctuary farm, and tell the authorities to take a flying leap."

As she lowered herself onto the old leather couch, Cliff rubbed his eyes and squinted at her.

"That's your intuitive side speaking, right?" he asked tenderly, "the one which says let consequences be damned, I'm acting on faith and Christian principals and all that radical stuff?"

"I guess so." Ruthalice cradled her hot mug with both hands and stared at the fire. "Why is basic human justice so darn hard to come by, Cliff? Gideon was a small boy when he got caught up in the Somali civil war. He managed to hang on by the skin of his teeth, get himself to the States, and finish college. I simply can't stand the idea of him being deported."

Her voice grew ragged as tears slid silently down her cheeks. She set her mug on the coffee table and blew her nose. Cliff replaced his glasses and warily sipped his cocoa. As the logs settled, a pop like a gunshot exploding made them both jump.

"Well, Sweetheart, if it's any consolation, I cannot imagine that our Professor Hopkins will sit idly by and allow the US government to get its hands on Gideon. It would feel like a betrayal of old Doc Martin's trust in his ability and commitment to keep the young man safe."

"I agree. Keeping promises and following through must be at the top of Curly's to-do list."

"You can add loyalty to that list, because in my humble opinion our Charles has become quite fond of Gideon Boseka." Cliff set his mug on the coffee table and turned toward Ruthalice. "But you know what troubles me about this whole sorry affair? At first, only Doc Martin and Charles and then recently the boss lady knew Gideon was in the basement, but since the fire, three more of us have been added to what was once a pretty exclusive list."

Cliff got up and jabbed the coals with the black poker lying on the hearth. "From where I sit, Ruthalice, there is no good way out of this refugee mess." A shower of sparks danced out of the logs. "I don't like anything about this right now."

"Cliff, you're scaring me," Ruthalice said, as he rejoined her on the couch.

"I'm simply trying to make sense of how a fire inexplicably breaks out in the Old Dean's House." He leaned over and kissed Ruthalice gently on the forehead.

Ruthalice took Cliff's head in both hands and returned his kiss. A half-hour later they were sound asleep, propping each other up like two old pillows. Somehow in the middle of the night, the M&Ms made their way down the back hallway and into bed.

## CHAPTER TWENTY-TWO

R uthalice's left arm swept lightly over the empty space now grown cold beside her and leapt out of bed. She stepped dutifully on the bathroom scale for her weight program's required weekly weigh-in and peered at the illuminated red numbers.

"Well, at least I'm headed in the right direction," she sighed, making a mental note of one hundred and eighty-two pounds. "But I'm still too much the traditionally built lady."

She pulled on pink sweatpants and matching sweatshirt with "Sleep Here When it Happens!" plastered across her ample bosom and followed the delicious smell of coffee straight through the living room into the kitchen. On her way back, she drew open the floor length drapes, preparing the room to receive the new day, then turned and headed for the green leather couch.

"You're sporting Packfield's town motto this morning, I see."

Ruthalice grinned. "When you said let's honeymoon in Monterey, California, I pictured sea and sand otters, not the earthquake epicenter of the USA, population eighteen."

As Ruthalice plopped down beside him, Cliff held his mug over the braided rug to avoid spilling hot liquid.

"But what a find, eh? Dozens of small earthquakes every single week, seismic instruments on every hillside and valley. Remember that cafe? I ordered The Big

One well done and you had Magnitude Six medium rare," Cliff chuckled, "with Aftershocks for dessert!"

"That was one of your better ideas, my dear Clifford. Who woulda thunk it'd turn out to be such a funky honeymoon location!" Ruthalice placed her slippered feet on the coffee table. "So, how long have you been up?"

"Oh, not very long." Cliff dropped this week's *Around Boone County* beside his wife's feet. "You up for the Saturday morning special?"

"Absolutely." Ruthalice got to her feet. "I'll go see what the hens laid yesterday."

She pulled her wool barn coat over the earthquake sweatshirt, tugged on a pair of rubber boots, and headed out the door, leaving Cliff happily banging around the kitchen gathering up the ingredients for his fabulous pancake and sausage breakfast.

After breakfast, feeling happily stuffed and fully charged, the M&Ms migrated to the bedroom.

"So what are you up to today, Sweetheart, anything in particular?" he asked, tugging the polka dot sheets and vermillion down coverlet over the king-size mattress. "Have you seen my work boots, by the way?"

Ruthalice scowled from the other side of the bed. "You're a big boy now, Clifford Mowry. Keep track of your own stuff."

Cliff bent over to check under the bed for his wandering boots and stood up clutching his left boot. He spotted the toe of the second one poking out from under the Carhart bib-overalls draped over the rocking chair in the corner. He held them high as a triumphant grin spread across his face.

"Now that I've successfully rounded up both boots, are you up for a hike? We haven't been along the creek in a long time."

"Beats raking leaves!"

Ruthalice tossed a water bottle and OSU ball cap at Cliff, tugged on her Emerick College knit hat, and headed out onto the wooden porch. They hiked across the pasture strewn with ironweed and dried milkweed pods, then started upstream following the stream bank. Ruthalice clung to the occasional overhanging branch, steadying herself to keep from tripping.

"Let's head to the bend and sit on that oak log," she said. "We can get through here."

Cliff stepped around her, lost his footing, and slid ingloriously into the creek.

"Damn that's cold," he shrieked, as water seeped through the boot and soaked his wool sock. "Watch out for that rock, Ruthalice, it's tippy."

"I see that." Cliff hopped around madly, shaking his sopping wet left foot. "You're gonna end up back in the water if you don't watch it," Ruthalice said, grabbing his arm.

Together they clambered up to the wide oak log. Lichens clung to its sides like empty, dirty plates. Ruthalice spread her wool shirt on the deeply scarred surface of the old tree and sat down. An enormous black crow cawed from the buckeye tree as a red-tailed hawk circled and whistled overhead. Soothed by the steady gurgle of creek water, Ruthalice leaned back and watched the raptor circle and soar, correcting its flight with a flap of its powerful wings. She ran her fingers down the stalk of a tall blade of grass, broke it in half, and stuck the sweet-tasting end in her mouth. The seed head bobbed up and down as she nibbled. Cliff sat on the ground, rested his back against the rough bark, and sighed as Ruthalice's fingers gently twisted his red curly hair.

"By the way, you haven't filled me in on the big conference with all the president's men—and ladies," he added quickly.

Ruthalice leaned back on her hands, enjoying the soft prickle of warm wood on her palms. She closed her eyes, and tilting her face back, began a blow-by-blow recitation of the preceding day's meeting.

"Hold on a minute, what's this about fireworks?"

"Somebody was storing firecrackers in the cubbyhole. Between the time the 911 call came in and the fire trucks arrived, the basement was burning like all get out."

Cliff wrestled his left foot out of the sodden boot and tugged at the sock. He grasped the cuff of his shirtsleeve and pulled it over his right hand then scrubbed his foot and toes until they were dry.

"Thank goodness Gideon kept his head and called the fire department. There aren't any basement windows, so it's conceivable that by the time anyone noticed smoke or flame, it would have been too late to save the Second Sister."

"The college owes Gideon an enormous amount of gratitude, but I suspect he will remain its secret, unsung hero." Ruthalice rubbed the wood chips from the palms of her hands, then flicked the mashed grass blade into the creek. "He was taking an incredible risk when he called the cops." She raised her legs and crossed them on the broad back of the log. "For some reason I have yet to understand, Angus kept insisting ad nauseam yesterday that nobody goes down into that basement anymore."

"How can he be so sure about that?"

"I don't know." Ruthalice offered her finger to the wooly worm caterpillar making its way across her thigh.

It quickly worked its way up and over her knuckle and down the other side. "He is partially correct, however, because Ernestine told Richard that no one from the alumni office has been in the basement since last June."

"However, we both know that's simply not true." Cliff laid the wet sock across the top of his boot and joined Ruthalice on the log. "You and I know two people who've been down there recently, Gideon and our elusive arsonist."

The great blue heron standing in the pool just beyond the bend slowly raised a skinny leg, set it silently back into the water, and struck. The legs of a large frog dangled from its beak as it raised its head.

"I'm just stating the obvious here, OK? First of all, Gideon did not stash fireworks in the basement of Penington Place, and secondly, our anonymous culprit went to great lengths to hide them, which leads me to conclude that he or she is well aware that possession of fireworks is illegal in this state."

Ruthalice let out a long, drawn-out sigh. "I can't stand the idea that somebody in our college community is to blame for this fire. I'm still rooting for a fuse box socket thingamajiggy shorting out."

"In the cubbyhole? That makes no sense whatsoever."

Ruthalice swatted at a black fly buzzing persistently around her face.

"So what have we got, Clifford? Spontaneous combustion?"

"You wish." He took her hand and kissed her fingers, then set it back on the log. "I'm wondering whose presence in the basement would go unnoticed."

"Gideon's, apparently," Ruthalice replied immediately. The heron dipped its knees, leaned forward, and

rose slowly into the sky. "The way this campus oper-
ates just about any normal looking human being could
come and go as they please, at least during office hours,
without anyone raising an eyebrow."

"Does anyone sit at the reception desk in the parlor
anymore?" Cliff asked.

"Nope, that position was eliminated when Quaker
Archives moved upstairs."

"That's what I thought. So the reality is, anyone
could mosey into the kitchen, descend the basement
stairs with a bag full of firecrackers tucked under their
arm, and go unnoticed." Cliff managed to swat the fly
as it finally landed on the top of Ruthalice's head. "We
keep coming back to who was in the basement Tuesday
night, don't we?"

Ruthalice straightened up and rubbed her lower
back. "Whew, it's time to start moving, Cliff. I'm getting stiff." She slid off the log. "Let's revisit what starts
a fire."

"OK, so what starts a fire?" Cliff pulled his boot
back on. "A match, a blow torch, lightning, a spark."

"An electrical short, but you ruled that out already.
Gideon's lantern. Oh, dear God, I hope that's not true!"

Ruthalice scratched her cheek and began to inch
her way along the bank. "A cigarette."

Cliff stopped lacing his boot.

"A cigarette. Of course, that's perfect." He dou-
ble-knotted the rawhide boot lace and got to his feet.
"So, now the question is, who smokes on campus?"

"Good heavens, Cliff, all kinds of people. But since
Emerick's a nonsmoking campus, nobody smokes out
in the open anymore, that's all."

"So, if I wanted to smoke, I'd head for an out-of-the
way place to do so."

"Like the basement of Penn Place."

"Especially after everyone had left for the day."

"In my very limited experience," Ruthalice began, "it's darn difficult to disguise the smell of cigarette smoke." She grinned at Cliff. "I know I for one nearly always got caught."

"And that's precisely why, my dear, our dastardly deed was done after hours and out of sight."

Ruthalice bent over and picked up a painted turtle sunning itself on a shiny flat rock at the edge of a small pool. It pulled its head and legs and tail into its shell. Its tightly closed eyes were just narrow slits in a black-and-yellow-striped face. "We all do that, don't we?" She gently touched the turtle's little pointed nose with her fingertip.

"We all do what?"

"Hide when we're feeling under siege or ashamed or are just plain too embarrassed to own up to something. We scurry off and go into hiding."

Cliff smiled down at her. "It's instinctual, Ruthalice. Threaten any of the invertebrates I work with, and they will disappear inside a shell or under a rock."

"We hide, thinking we're safe." Ruthalice gently placed the painted turtle back on its rock. It scrambled back into the water, dove to the muddy bottom, and vanished. "God, you are my hiding place, my shelter in the time of storm."

"And my fortress." Cliff extended his hand and helped her up the bank.

The M&Ms hiked back across the field as dark gray clouds began to build on the western horizon.

# CHAPTER TWENTY-THREE

It started raining shortly after midnight. By four-thirty, the ceaseless drumming on the tin roof drove sleep away. Ira fumbled for his slippers in the dimly lit room, wrapped himself in a well-worn flannel bathrobe, and went to stand beside the water-streaked window. He crossed to the ladderback chair beside the bedroom door and perched on the brown, wicker seat. Unable to silence the chatter in his mind, he lumbered back to his feet and peered once again into the deserted, rain-soaked street. The enormity of his wife's deteriorating condition and the thought of speaking about what he had done joined forces to overwhelm him.

"What on earth is the matter, Ira? You've been pacing the floor for hours."

Ira Tibbetts turned from the window and went to stand beside the bed.

"I didn't mean to disturb you, Nora." He took her frail, deformed hand and held it gently between his sturdy, rough ones. "I've got a lot on my mind this morning." He smiled, "You know me, I don't think very well sitting down."

Nora favored him with what remained of the smile that won his heart nearly forty years ago. He studied her face as she fumbled with the white afghan coverlet strewn with embroidered red roses. Remembering a long-ago reprimand, Ira resisted the persistent urge to straighten the bedding for her. *I can still manage to cover myself up, Ira. I'm dependent on you for nearly everything else. Please don't take what little independence remains away from me as well.* At least for now, on this miserably bleak morning, Ira was willing to share the burden of his wife's rheumatoid arthritis and honor her request.

Nora arranged the coverlet and nodded toward the bedroom's solitary chair.

"Husband, you're frightening me. Turn on a light, sit down, and talk to me."

Ira placed the ladderback chair at the foot of her bed, straightened its yellow-striped cushion, and sat down. He gazed around the spare bedroom where his wife was living out the last of her days. Nora's niece, Polly, did the weekly housekeeping and insisted on flinging the window wide open, regardless of the weather. It was Polly who turned the dull, white walls a soft yellow and hung white, Wal-Mart café curtains in the window. Ira was pleased with the tiny room's clean coziness and welcoming warmth. The guild ladies from St. Mary's Catholic Church who came by every Monday morning to drop off a copy of the church bulletin along with a tape of the sermon, were frequently heard to comment that Nora Tibbetts's room never had the old-folks-nursing-home smell one might expect in the room of someone in her condition.

Nora stifled the scream welling up inside her as she silently watched the tears slither down her husband's wrinkled, pudgy cheeks and drop on the faded flannel fabric of his bathrobe.

"Nora," he pulled a red bandana from his robe pocket and wiped his nose, "I have done a terrible thing." He began to pick at the edges of the handkerchief, slowly unraveling the hem. "I fell behind in my work again." He raised his head and stared into her pale blue eyes. "My assignment was to service the furnaces Tuesday night, but that old Bryant in Fox Hall required new parts, so it took much longer than I expected it to."

A wrinkle creased Nora's pale white forehead. "I don't understand."

"It was after nine before I finished in Fox Hall. By then I was hungry, so I went to Subway for supper. I knew I had to finish cleaning both furnaces before Wednesday morning or Mr. Bailey would be all over me, so I went back to campus around ten o'clock to take care of Penington Place."

Rubbing his eyes, Ira slumped in the chair. He placed a hand on each thigh in an effort to quiet the involuntary twitches which made his legs jump. In a voice heavy with exhaustion, he said, "I finished up around midnight and came home."

Nora tugged the edges of the afghan until the fabric lay smooth across her narrow body. The task complete, she rested her arms at her side.

"Ira Tibbetts, how can I help you if you won't tell me the entire story?"

Ira got to his feet, upsetting the wooden chair in the process. He put it back in its place beside the bedroom door and walked to the closet. He pulled the closest white shirt off its hanger, slipped it on, and began buttoning from the neck down.

Nora watched her husband slip on a pair of black trousers. The long-suppressed scream of despair lay coiled just below the surface. With all the certainty of the dying, Nora knew she could not contain the anguish much longer.

"Tell me where you are going."

Ira ran a green plastic comb through his thin brown hair, then clipped a paisley bowtie to his collar. "I'm going to confession." He pulled himself up straight, stared into the mirror, and addressed the ashen face reflecting back at him from the bed. "I'm going to talk with Father Paul. I have a sin to confess."

"Husband, we have never kept secrets from each other. You must tell me also."

"I am smoking again."

"Oh, thank you, Jesus." Nora closed her eyes and inhaled. "I was afraid you were still shoplifting." She opened her eyes. "Father Paul will forgive you, my dear Ira. Smoking is only a human weakness and failing not a cardinal sin."

Ira tucked a clean handkerchief into the breast pocket of his shirt. "It is still raining cats and dogs out there, so I'll take the car. If I get to church before seven-thirty, Father will hear my confession right away." He tucked his billfold into the right pocket of his trousers. "I plan to stay for morning mass."

He felt Nora relax as he kissed her gently on the check.

"How about I stop at the OQ Bakery and get some of those custard-filled long johns for breakfast?"

"Sounds sinfully delightful," she replied, "and it gives me something to look forward to this morning."

Nora listened to his footsteps retreating down the hallway. She waited for the front door to slam, then began to pray,

"Lord Jesus Christ

Son and Word of the Living God

By the prayer of your most pure Mother and all the Saints

Have mercy on us and save us."

## CHAPTER TWENTY-FOUR

The steady rain hammered the shingles at Horse-feathers Farm. Water ran along the eaves and gushed out the drainpipes onto the soggy grass. A loose shutter banged against the bedroom wall as the wind picked up. Ruthalice leapt out of bed and dashed to the window, grabbed the cold metal handle and began cranking the window shut. An icy mist sprayed her face. Shivering, she headed straight to the bathroom, yanked the nearest towel off the stack by the door, and furiously rubbed her face and arms.

"Are you staying up?" The groggy voice came from Cliff's side of the bed.

"I'll never get back to sleep now. Besides it's nearly seven." She kissed his warm forehead. "Do you want the radio on?" A sleepy grunt answered her question.

Accompanied by the twangy sounds of old-time gospel, Ruthalice sang her way across the living room and into the kitchen. "Shall we gather at the river, the be-u-tiful, be-u-tiful, river?" She was busy scribbling and erasing when Cliff ambled into the kitchen an hour later, his flannel sleeping shirt barely reaching his knees.

"Whatcha working on so diligently this First Day morning?" he asked, pouring a cup of coffee. He crossed the room and stood at the end of the table. "Scoot over," he said, sliding in beside her on the cushion-covered bench.

"I promised Mike Peters I'd have my part of the new EC publicity brochure ready by the end of the week, but since I'm just getting started on it, I'm attempting to make up for the error of my ways this morning!"

"Let's see what you've got so far."

Oakes Quarry was settled in 1821 by two Quaker brothers, Obadiah and Sterling Emerick, who joined the large settlement of Friends (Quakers) migrating from North Carolina to Ohio to escape the institution of slavery. The brothers began farming and built a functional house of stone. In 1823 Sterling married Sarah Cluxton in a simple Quaker wedding. Hannah Elizabeth Emerick, the youngest of their seven children, founded Emerick College in 1872 as a school for women, the only institution of its kind for hundreds of miles around. Ms. Emerick taught English, French, and Art History, and four years after she courageously shared her vision with the town council, the Emerick School for Women graduated its first class.

"An excellent summation, Ruthalice. I've only got two corrections."

Ruthalice put on her best Cheshire cat grin. "I'm all ears."

"OK, their wedding was in 1824 instead of '23, and technically, Hannah was the youngest of *eight* children, as the one born before her died at two months of age."

Ruthalice marked the changes with her trusty, red ink pen. "I'm going to add that Miss Hannah was the first woman to be recorded as a minister in our neck of the Quaker woods."

Cliff nodded. "Oh, by the way, you'll be interested to know that it's now official. WKOA reported this morning that exploding firecrackers started the Penington fire."

Ruthalice looked up from her yellow pad. "Really."

"The newscaster didn't elaborate, but I think that

effectively rules out Gideon's lantern."

"Thank God for that." She wrinkled her forehead. "I think Gideon's exact words were, 'I always turn light out before I go.'" Ruthalice turned slightly and laid her hand on Cliff's arm. "Remember Gideon telling us he smelled smoke the minute he opened the coal bin door..."

"and immediately jumped down into the basement, lit the lantern, grabbed as many belongings as he could get his hands on, scrambled back out, and called the fire department from the campus emergency phone in front of Harvey Library."

Ruthalice laid her pen diagonally on the pad of paper in front of her. "It took real courage to stand under the security light in full view of anybody who happened to look out a window or wander by."

"It was the middle of the night."

"It was still a pretty gutsy thing to do." She looked at Cliff. "Why are you shaking your head?"

"I'm beginning to think Ernestine hasn't got a clue about what goes on in that building."

Ruthalice shot Cliff a bemused look. "You're probably right, but we're going in circles, and it's making me crazy."

Cliff moved around to his side of the breakfast nook. "Well, my dear, I don't know about you, but I'm ready to eat."

"I need to accomplish something this morning," Ruthalice said, springing into action. "Cold cereal or cinnamon oatmeal?"

"Oh, I don't care—whichever's easier for you."

Ruthalice retrieved a bag of Cheerios, a jug of milk, and two handmade, stoneware bowls. She poured milk into her bowl and patted down the bobbing stray loops of cereal with the back of her spoon.

"Cliff, I've got an idea," she said, looking at him across the table. "Since it's such a lousy day, weather-wise, let's invite Charles and Gideon out for the afternoon. We'll light a fire and watch football or NASCAR or whatever's on TV, and they can stay for dinner as well. What do you think?"

"That's a wonderful idea," Cliff said, a warm smile covering his face. "And by the way, that's why I love you, Ms. Ruthalice Michels. You think of things that would never occur to me."

"I hope Charles will be OK bringing Gideon out of the house in broad daylight."

"We won't know until we ask, will we."

Ruthalice buttered her raisin toast. "Tell Charles we'll be back from meeting for worship by noon, so come any time after that and plan to spend the rest of the day."

"Consider it done, my dear."

Cliff licked the peach jam off his fingers and reached for the cell phone lying on top of the *New York Times* crossword puzzle book as Ruthalice headed for the shower. A few minutes later he knocked rambunctiously on the shower door.

"Come on in," she replied, moving out of the way as her buck-naked husband stepped through the opening and quickly closed the door behind him. She shoved the bar of soap into his hands. "So, what did Curly say?"

"A jolly good idea! Says it'd do 'em good to get out." He chuckled as the water cascaded down his soapy chest. "Sounds like our old campus curmudgeon's having to make considerable adjustments to his solitary, bachelor, weekend routine."

## CHAPTER TWENTY-FIVE

"Are you coming, Gideon?" Charles growled impatiently. "It's nearly half-past. Ruthalice and Clifford were expecting us at one."

Getting no response, he clumped down the basement steps. When he reached the bottom, he saw Gideon in the middle of the room, shaking his blanket, a puzzled look on his face.

"Lose something, old chap?"

"I can only find one flip-flop, Professor Curly." He picked up his shirt and trousers in turn, giving each one a shake. "I lost one."

"You don't need flip-flops, it's pouring outside."

"I do not have good rain shoes. Look."

He held up two ragged, dirty tennis shoes with holes in both toes.

"Forget the flip-flops. We'll buy a new pair of shoes at the Wal-Mart on our way out of town." A look of uneasiness crossed his young friend's face. "Oh, that's right. I can't take you into Wally, can I? Where is your head these days, Charles?" He waved both hands in exasperation. "Never mind. Just come on, Gideon. I'll just take one of your loafers in with me." Without waiting for a reply, he plodded back up the stairs, Gideon following meekly on behind.

Forty-five minutes later, the improbable duo chugged out of town in the little VW, its windshield wipers operating at full speed. Gideon threaded the laces of his new red and white Nikes and inhaled the new-shoe smell. He slipped them on and turned his feet from side to side.

"Thank you for socks, too, Professor Curly." His soft, lyrical voice made the words sing. "You are my friend." Gideon's stare flitted between the windshield and the side window. "Look at the cattle out there," he said with delight, pointing at a herd of Black Angus grazing behind acres of field fence, seemingly oblivious to the driving rain. "I like cattle."

"Do you miss Doolow?" The professor's voice was surprisingly gentle. "I jolly well miss the English countryside." He lifted his right hand off the steering wheel, waving it aloft.

"'The sun above the mountain's head,
A freshening luster mellow;
Through all the long green fields has spread,
His first sweet evening yellow.'"

Charles chuckled appreciatively, "Ah, Wordsworth."

"Wordsworth? What is this Wordsworth?"

"Who, my boy, who! William Wordsworth is the Lake District poet, and in my humble opinion, the best of our British bards."

Charles slowed at the bottom of the driveway and maneuvered the wheezing little Beetle up the winding gravel lane of Horsefeathers Farm.

"Well, Gideon, we've arrived at our destination." Shoulders hunched, Charles sprinted for the front porch. He turned his head and hollered, "Come on, Gideon, it's bucketing down out here!"

Gideon stuffed the brand-new socks into his brand-new shoes, clutched them against his chest, and began to hop over puddles in his bare feet. He joined the professor on the wide wooden porch just as Clifford flung the door open.

"Come on in. If this keeps up, old Noah's going to have to start building again." He stepped aside as the two men crowded through the front door. "Here let me take your coats," glancing at Gideon's feet he added, "and get a towel for you, my young friend."

Charles headed straight for the handsome Victorian chair to the right of the fireplace and sat down. Gideon edged his way into the middle of the room, his eyes never leaving the large, plate-glass window which dominated the west wall.

"We're all alone out here, Gideon," Ruthalice said gently. "Please, come and sit by the fire. You must be cold."

"In Somalia it is always too dry, so we are very happy when it rain."

Gideon moved to the green leather couch and perched like a cat poised to slink away at the slightest sign of danger. Cliff handed Gideon a soft yellow towel and sat down beside him.

"Is that Africa?" Gideon nodded toward the small watercolor hanging above the claw-foot dining room table.

"Yes, that is Kenya, the Rift Valley to be exact. A Quaker friend of ours, Mateau Ketoyo painted it. I led worship one Sunday morning at Nairobi Friends Meeting. The pastor gave me the painting as a thank-you gift." Ruthalice smiled. "I love those sprawling acacia trees and the blue African sky that seems to go on forever."

"Mr. Mateau is very good artist."

Like lines forgotten in the first act of the play, the opening chit chat slipped into an awkward silence.

"Gideon," Ruthalice said, clearing a space in the middle of the coffee table. "I am woefully ignorant about your country and its geography, so I went on the internet this morning." She placed a piece of paper on the glass surface. "I've printed out a map of Somalia. Would you show us where you used to live?"

Gideon slipped off the sofa onto his knees, gave the map a quarter turn, and pointed to the upper left. "This is my town I grow up in, Doolow. See, it is where Ethiopia, Kenya, and Somalia borders come together."

"Ah, yes, the Mandera Triangle," Charles intoned. The others gave him a startled look. "The tri-border area is known as the Mandera Triangle," Charles explained, "where a man's wealth and status are dependent upon the number of cattle he owns. It is the most desperately poor area on the entire continent."

"Professor Curly is right." Gideon ran his finger down the map. "Here is Chisimaio where my cousin Luther come from down on Indian Ocean, about one hundred kilometers south of Mogadishu."

He sat back on his haunches and stared at the map. "There is no peace in the triangle area of my country. There is too much fighting in our capital city. Many thousands of people get killed in Mogadishu, and now come the terrorists," he added bitterly, "who kill anybody they don't like."

"Until 1941 Somalia was known as Italian Somaliland. The Italians occupied Chisimaio." Cliff tapped the middle of the map. "I remember reading about the 1995 siege of Baidoa. Hundreds of innocent civilians were killed in that siege. My nephew was serving in the Marines at the time, and when fighting broke out in September, the family worried he'd be sent to Somalia."

Gideon grasped the edges of the coffee table with both hands. "My mother and my baby sister Corinne, they are slaughtered in Baidoa." He began rocking back and forth. "They go visit my auntie. My grandmother is not well, so mama and my sister go to help. The soldiers firebomb the house—" His voice trailed off.

"May your dear ones rest in peace, Gideon." Ruthalice gently covered his hand with hers. "Three more innocent victims of war. We and God know their names."

"A classic case of being in the wrong place at the wrong time," Charles said. "It's bloody awful."

Gideon wadded up the tissue Ruthalice held out to him, then cleared his throat. "My father is part of resistance movement in Somalia. US soldiers shoot and kill him two years before my mama died." The logs shifted in the fireplace. "There is always civil war in my country," Gideon continued, "and much fighting in the streets of Mogadishu."

"The Transitional Federal Government in Somalia is totally incapable of governing the country." Charles's voice rose as he switched into lecture mode, the living room his classroom. "The United Nations reports that 1.8 million Somalis are currently in danger of dying from malnourishment. Four hundred thousand Somalis have been displaced from their homes. And now the government, such as it is, has Al Shabab to deal with, which is waging a deadly insurgency in the south and center of the country. I read yesterday that Al Shabab announced the execution of five men accused of spying for the US, British, and Somali intelligence agencies."

"I saw that story as well," Cliff said. "According to eyewitnesses, the men were tied to poles and shot after a self-proclaimed judge sentenced them to death." He leaned forward and rested his elbows on his knees. "I also heard on NPR that Doctors without Borders has withdrawn all their volunteers because of threats against their medical staff. Some of their clinics have been destroyed."

"And the waters off the Somali coast are rife with pirates." Charles crossed his arms. "No captain is willing to sail or dock without being afforded naval protection. The situation is untenable."

Ruthalice joined Cliff on the couch with Gideon between them. As the logs finally settled into a warm steady glow, a somber silence descended on the little circle of friends.

"Remind me again, Gideon," Ruthalice said, laying her hand on his wrist. "How did you get to Emerick College?"

"My father dies in September 1993." Gideon wiped his mouth with the back of his hand. "Ten thousand people die between June and October 1993 in resistance to UN and US forces in Somalia."

His voice dropped so low his audience strained to hear. "My mother and my sister Corinne are killed in September 1995. The war lord Aideed was fighting for power." He paused, "How you say, Professor Curly? Aideed is one bad ass man!" A look of defiance sparked in Gideon's eyes, then faded into resignation. "Six hundred of Aideed armed guerrillas fight their way into Baidoa. They raid and bomb my auntie's house."

"After my mother die, I stay in Doolow and finish school, but there is much hunger and no jobs, so I go to Mogadishu to find how to leave Somalia. I am orphan living in streets always try to not get killed. I eat a cat."

Ruthalice winced. *First dogs, now cats.*

"An old man strangles three cats, he see I am hungry and give me one to eat. It is only thing I eat in five days."

"We war refugees cannot afford to be picky, can we, Gideon?" Charles said quietly. Their eyes met briefly before Charles looked away.

"Finally, I go to the mission house to sleep. That is where Dr. Martin meets me."

Charles seemed to snap out of some distant reverie and took up the story.

"Terrell Martin had recently retired from college teaching and was engaged in humanitarian work for the United Nations in Somalia. He met Gideon on the mission's charity soup line. He and our friend here spent a good many hours together as it turns out. Martin took quite a shine to you, Gideon."

A dazzling smile swept across Gideon's face. "Professor Martin say come to USA with me. 'How I do that?' I ask, and he say, 'We get you papers.' So, we go to embassy and get a visa and a passport. 'You are good college material,' he says." Gideon held up his right arm, his forefinger pointed toward the ceiling. "Gideon must go to Emerick College and make a future for himself in America.'"

"And by Jove, old Martin was spot on that time, eh, Clifford?"

"I should say so!" Cliff grinned broadly. "Gideon Boseka learned to tell his clams from his mussels and snails. You were the one student I could always count on to be excited about wading knee-deep in Brush Creek. Neither rain nor snow nor dark of night keeps a true malacologist from his appointed field trip."

"I love mollusks!" Gideon said. "Ohio has unusual number of species of freshwater clams. It is hot spot for clam biodiversity. That is what Professor Clifford teach me."

Ruthalice clapped her hands. "Bravo, Gideon. Well done."

"All right, all right, that's enough!" Cliff said. With a sweep of his arm he indicated the television at the opposite end of the room. "The Bengals game comes on in ten minutes."

Gideon scrambled to his feet. "Oh, good, American football." He looked back at Ruthalice, who remained seated, her legs stretched out under the coffee table. "Thank you, Miss Ruthalice for getting map. You are very kind."

"You're quite welcome, Gideon." She got to her feet and placed the printout map on the mantle. "Popcorn anyone?"

Three hours later, thoroughly satisfied by the Cincinnati Bengals' 24-17 win over the Chicago Bears, and full of lamb stew, they lingered around the dining room table until the last of the coffee and ice cream had disappeared.

Charles abruptly shoved his chair back from the dining room table and stood up. "Come on, Gideon, it's time for us to hit the road. This old boy's ready for bed."

The M&Ms stood on the porch as the VW's headlights bounced down the hill and disappeared into the drippy, moonless night.

"I've grown quite fond of Gideon," Ruthalice said softly.

"They do make quite the pair, those two, don't they, Sweetheart," Cliff replied.

He closed the door and joined Ruthalice who stood in front of the fireplace, aimlessly moving the coals around with the iron poker.

"I can picture little Curly huddled up on a pile of blankets deep in the Underground in the middle of London, surrounded by hundreds of frightened neighbors and strangers." She slipped her left hand into Cliff's. "Then years later and half a world away, a skinny little Somali boy named Gideon Boseka is forced to scavenge through the alleys and city dumps, running and hiding from the killing."

Ruthalice drew the long brown braid over her shoulder and began to rub the tip against her cheek. "And here we were, another world away, you all safe and sound up here on Horsefeathers Farm, happily dispensing biological knowledge to college students, and me, a single mom trying to balance raising a son and managing a retreat center." She leaned against Cliff as he put his arm around her shoulders. "How can we possibly feel even the tiniest bit of their terror?"

Ruthalice wiped her upper lip with her right sleeve as her nose began to drip. "I simply can't fathom what it's like to be on the run, never looking back, terrified of getting caught by the wrong people." She drew a deep breath. "Dear God," she moaned, "these were just innocent children whose only mistake was to be born in the middle of a war they had absolutely nothing to do with."

She turned and stared through the rain-streaked window out into the pitch-black night. "'Remember the alien amongst you for you also are sojourners in the land,'" Ruthalice quoted softly. "You know, Cliff, until Friday night, the alien in my midst had no face, no name, no story to share, but now—"

Cliff placed his hands on her cheeks and turned her face toward him. "Isn't it in Matthew where Jesus says when we welcome the stranger, we also welcome him?"

He wrapped his strong arms around her and drew her close. "I am thanking God for all the Terrell Martins and Charles Hopkins out there in this crazy, out-of-kilter world."

"Me, too," Ruthalice said, rubbing her damp cheek against his sweater vest. "Me, too."

# CHAPTER TWENTY-SIX

"OK, that completes our survey of the major prophets. Are there any questions?" Ruthalice dropped the chalk in the tray and smiled what she hoped was a smile of encouragement. From the back row, a student tentatively raised his hand, his face all but invisible under a Yankees cap.

"Yes, Brian."

"Do we have to know the names of these guys?"

"Yes, and you also need to be able to describe their basic message to the Hebrew people." This time, Professor Michels fixed the class with an expectant look over the top of her glasses, *library matron style*. "And the major prophets are—" She paused, waiting for responses from the floor.

"Isaiah, Jeremiah, Ezekiel," Amanda Coffin volunteered from the front row.

"Exactly." Ruthalice glanced at the clock, then pointed at the chalkboard. "Read the textbook assignment plus these passages in Amos, Micah, Hosea, and Daniel for Wednesday."

The sound of zippers, cell phone tones, and miscellaneous grumbling about too much reading signaled the end of class. "Wish I had the nerve to play my air violin," Ruthalice muttered under her breath to their retreating backsides.

"Ruthalice, I have a question."

"Of course, Amanda, let's go down to my office."

Ruthalice dropped her books on the cluttered desktop and plugged the electric teakettle into the wall socket between *The Geneva Bible* and *Volume A-D of the Interpreter's Dictionary* on the row of shelves second from the bottom. Amanda set her backpack on the carpet, took a pen from her jacket pocket, and dropped onto the orange chair.

"I'm not sure I understand the differences between Jeremiah and Isaiah well enough to talk intelligently about them." She flipped open a college-lined spiral notebook. "Do you have time to help me?"

"Sure," Ruthalice responded enthusiastically, and for the next half hour the two women sipped tea and discussed biblical justice and the role of prophecy in the Hebrew Testament.

"By the way, what does it mean to love my neighbor as myself?" Amanda cocked her head to one side and slipped a strand of auburn hair behind her ear. "I guess what I am asking is what am I supposed to actually *do?*" She paused, a mischievous twinkle in her eyes, "I'm pretty sure it does not mean I can hop in bed with all the good-looking ones. I doubt Jesus had that in mind."

"Good heavens!" Ruthalice raised her eyebrows in mock horror, "I should say not. But your question is an oldie-but-goodie." Ruthalice picked up her Bible. "What does Isaiah have to say about how we are to take care of each other?"

Amanda stared at her instructor. "Well, you said that Isaiah said that God says—" her laugh interrupted her recitation, "That's getting to be awfully third hand information, Ruthalice!"

Ruthalice shrugged her shoulders. "Give it a try," she replied, an expression of "that's-the-way-it-goes-sometimes" resting lightly on her face.

"Well, God says in chapter fifty-eight no more burnt offerings, no more charred sheep and goats. I don't need them anymore. Let's do things differently from now on."

"I believe you've nailed it." Ruthalice leaned back and smiled. "Chapter fifty-eight is pretty heady stuff, Amanda. Yahweh is really gung-ho on justice as an acceptable sacrifice."

The young woman ran her eyes and her finger quickly down the onion-skin page, nodding vigorously as she read. "Let the oppressed go free, clothe the naked and feed them bread." She looked up her eyes shining. "I think I'm starting to get the answer to my original question."

"What does it mean to love thy neighbor?"

"Yup, it's a do unto others kind of thing isn't it?"

"Said another way, I'll help remove your yoke and carry your burden if you'll do the same for me."

Amanda stood up and stretched. "Thanks so much for the private tutorial lesson, Ruthalice," she said, tucking the bottom of her shirt back into her blue jeans. "My Johnny's been home with the measles since Thursday, and it seems like the only time I can study is in the middle of the night."

"College is challenging enough when you're nineteen, single, and supposedly without a care in the world. I don't know how you single moms do it."

"I wouldn't know about that," Amanda snorted. "By the time I was nineteen, I had a one-year-old, with another one in the oven, which was just about the time my no-good boyfriend decided to cut and run." She checked her appearance in the mirror hanging on the back of the office door. "Mom helps out so there's generally enough for us to get by on. Then there's always my pals at the food pantry."

Ruthalice reached around her and grasped the door-knob. "Come back anytime, Amanda. My door's always open."

"I know, and I will." She slipped in behind two parents and their daughter dutifully following the guide from the Admissions Office down the hallway.

"We just passed the Office of Campus Ministry on our right," the student guide intoned. "The Quaker meeting room at the end of the hall is where Oakes Quarry Friends Meeting holds unprogrammed worship. That means they don't have a pastor," she clarified as the little group shuffled on past and out of earshot.

Ruthalice sat at her desk replaying her conversations with Cliff over the weekend. She picked up the faculty/staff directory and pictured each face as she thumbed through the bright orange pages, trying to recall which ones she'd ever seen smoking a cigarette.

# CHAPTER TWENTY-SEVEN

L ynn Lawson watched Richard walk slowly up the corridor and drape his wet coat over the wooden wall peg behind the office door. She waited until he finished running through the raft of message and appointment slips on his desk, then came to stand quietly beside him.

"Angus Bailey wants a word."

"I saw him come out of the men's room on my way in."

"He says he's found something you ought to know about. It's just one surprise after another, isn't it?" she observed wryly as Richard fingered her handwritten note from her conversation with the fire chief. "It doesn't feel like there's a satisfactory end in sight."

"You're referring to the much sought after and highly prized 'light at the end of the tunnel' are you, Lynn? I just pray we're not sitting on a bombshell that's about to explode. Send Angus in, and get me a fresh cup of coffee while you're at it, will you please?" He cringed as his secretary unceremoniously dumped the cold dregs into his prize spider plant. "You're sure that's good for the plant?"

"Absolutely. They say it's good for the soil."

"Ah yes, the all-knowing 'they.'" Richard scratched his eyebrow with a well-manicured index finger. "By the way, when do I have to leave for my meeting in Columbus?"

"Your appointment's at one, so I'd say, what, eleven-thirty."

Richard pulled the leather chair out from under the desk and sat down. "Ask Evelyn to come by the office when she's ready to go."

Angus Bailey was waiting impatiently in the outer office for Lynn's OK. At her signal, he marched through the door and closed it firmly behind him. "Take a look at this, Richard," he said, thrusting a large brown envelope at the president.

He remained standing at the corner of the desk while Richard unwound the string from two red cardboard clasps and lifted the flap. "Good heavens, Angus, where did this come from?" he asked pulling out a black flip-flop. He sniffed the rubber sole and sneezed. "Whew, it's smoky."

"Bingo!" Angus thumped down in one of the chairs across the desk from Richard. He draped an arm over the chairback and regarded the president with a look of supreme satisfaction on his face. "One of my student crew members found it yesterday afternoon when they were cleaning up the Penn Place cellar. After they'd hauled out all that scorched furniture, they swept the floor and discovered this flip-flop under a pile of old rags in the coal bin at the southeast corner of the building."

"What coal bin?"

"Remember the original furnace?" The president gave a vague nod. "Well there's a small room in that corner of the basement with a half wall I'd say is probably four feet high, between the old furnace, which is still there by the way, and the rest of the basement. It was used as a coal bin back in the day. The flip-flop was shoved in a corner of that little back room." Angus rubbed his hands together. "Richard, we find the owner of this flip-flop and we've got our arsonist."

The president held the sandal up and turned it over. "I'd say it's way too old to be wearable. Just look at the cracks. It probably dates way back to the days when students held club meetings down there. Nobody missed it, so it just stayed put." He handed the flip-flop back to the director of the facilities, then wiped his hands on the white handkerchief he pulled from his pants pocket. "I can't imagine anyone's worn it for years."

"Well, I'm here to respectfully disagree with you, Richard. Barbara Carroll told me this morning student clubs haven't met in Penington since the early seventies. There's no way that flip-flop is forty odd years old."

"Did you know the flip-flop was introduced to the US after the Second World War when our soldiers brought them back from Japan and began wearing them?" Richard gave Angus a satisfied smile. "A bit of trivia on an otherwise dreary Monday morning."

The two men exchanged a guarded stare. Richard rested his elbows on the top of his desk and removed his glasses.

"Indulge me a bit here, Angus." The president stuck one eyeglass stem into his mouth and began lightly rubbing it back and forth against his teeth. "Check your duty roster and see if one of your personnel might have been in Penn sometime early last week."

Angus took his cell phone from his jacket pocket. "Judy, get the duty roster out for last Monday and Tuesday nights. No, I'll wait." He watched Richard replace his glasses and start tapping a pencil on the smooth mahogany surface of his executive desk. "Oh really? Doesn't tell us a whole heck of a lot though, does it?"

Angus lay the cell phone on his right thigh. "Ira Tibbetts was assigned the fall inspection of the furnaces on Tuesday. He clocked out at 9 p.m., indicating he had completed the work in both Fox and Penn."

A look of concern slipped across Angus's narrow face. His dark brown eyes traced the pattern on the Persian rug under their feet.

"What's got you puzzled over there, Angus?"

"I hate saying anything bad about one of my people, and I know Tibbetts has a lot on his plate these days what with his wife's sickly condition. You do know about Nora's condition?" Richard laid his pencil on the desk blotter and nodded. "I've tended to look the other way when he comes in late of a morning and when he uses the shop phone to call home four or five times a day, but—" Angus cleared his throat.

"But Ira isn't carrying his own weight anymore," Richard suggested gently.

"He's put on a good twenty pounds this year. These last couple of weeks he hasn't been applying himself enough to finish his job assignments on time." Angus stared past Richard's shoulder at the empty wall. "I've been giving him verbal warnings since Labor Day, but last Friday I issued a formal, written warning letter. I informed him that another sloppy job or one left undone, and I'll be forced to let him go."

"This is never easy, is it, Angus, especially in a case like this. Tibbetts has enormous demands and burdens at home." Richard caught the supervisor's eye. "It almost feels like cruel and unusual punishment."

"Ira has served Emerick College for nearly thirty years," Angus said, getting to his feet, "and for what it's worth, I can't image he's got anything to do with this fire." He set his jaw and turned toward the door. "As far as I'm concerned, Ira signed out at 9 p.m. and went home. End of story."

"The timecard confirms he signed out at nine,"

Richard agreed solemnly, "but until one of us talks with him, we can't be one hundred percent certain he went directly home."

Angus froze halfway to the door. "Why wouldn't he go straight home? He hates to leave Nora alone, especially at night." Their eyes met. "I'll call him in and talk with him myself," Angus said. "Do you want to keep that flip-flop? Maybe the police will want it," he added half-heartedly.

"Yes, I'll keep it and inform Chief Turner," Richard replied. His mind still with the faithful old handyman, he got slowly to his feet and came around the desk. "Does Ira have any family care or sick leave left?"

"Personnel's been more than generous in this case, but in a word, no. Tibbetts has used up all his sick and vacation days and then some."

"I was afraid of that." Richard opened the door and patted Angus on the right shoulder. "I know you can and will handle this, Angus. If I can be of any help, let me know."

The president glanced at the wall clock, picked up the desk phone, and dialed.

"I'll tell Chief about the flip-flop, sir," the female voice replied courteously. "I'm sure he'll want to follow up with you."

Two hours later Dean Feller arrived in Lynn's office looking just a little "last year" in a knee-length, plaid wool coat. "Off to Columbus," Richard informed his secretary. "I should be back in the office by nine tomorrow morning."

## CHAPTER TWENTY-EIGHT

A drippy gloom enveloped the campus when Ira Tibbetts arrived in his battered Ford pickup and logged in at eight-thirty. The remaining red and orange leaves hung limp and soggy as if the energy to wave and dance had been driven out of them by the cold, persistent rain. Ten windows in Douglas Resident Hall had required caulking, but now with the last window prepared for winter, Ira tossed the empty cardboard tubes into the dumpster and let the heavy lid drop down with a clang. He was headed back to the college maintenance van when his supervisor flagged him down. The ensuing parking-lot conversation left Ira troubled and uneasy, like a ship torn loose from its mooring.

As he side-stepped a shallow puddle nestled in a low spot in the pavement, Ira spotted the campus minister striding down Wood Avenue. He watched her chat with two students shoveling leaves out of the street drain, then bend over and pick up a bright red leaf. She climbed the porch steps, gave the umbrella a vigorous shake, and disappeared inside Frame Meetinghouse.

"You must speak with someone at the college, brother Ira, to someone who will listen without judgment," Father Paul had instructed him as he knelt in the confessional. "You cannot carry the burden of your fear alone. The weight of a secret grows lighter when shared."

Ira returned the tools to their proper places in the maintenance shed and checked his watch. Judy wasn't at the secretary's desk, so he stopped long enough to give his wife a call. Fifteen minutes later Ira stood outside the Office of Campus Ministry, took a deep breath, and knocked.

"Come on in," Ruthalice hollered over her shoulder. She swung her desk chair around and got to her feet. "Ira Tibbetts, long time no see!" She shook his hand, then drew him inside and closed the door. "Have a seat. Can I get you something to drink?"

"No thank you," Ira said, as he shuffled toward the orange armchair.

"So, Ira, what's on your mind?"

Ruthalice crossed her legs at the ankles and waited for her visitor to take the next step. Ira lowered his head and studied his fingers compulsively curling and uncurling as they lay in his lap.

"There is something weighing heavy on my mind I'd like to share." He cleared his throat. "Since you're a minister and all."

His gaze drifted from his lap to the top of Ruthalice's boots. "Angus Bailey stopped me in the parking lot this morning," he began in a soft, clear voice, "and asked me about signing out Tuesday night. Angus has never questioned my timecard before, so I couldn't figure out why he asked me did I go straight home." Ira frowned. "I told him yes, of course, I went home. I reminded him how sick and frail my Nora is." He twitched and shifted in his seat. "Angus just stared at me. He didn't question me or nothing. Then he dismissed me. But you see, Ruthalice, I didn't go right home Tuesday night." Ira's eyes moved to her right shoulder and flickered as something shifted inside. "After I signed out, I went to Penington Place."

"You were in Penn Tuesday night?" Ruthalice asked, struggling to keep the growing apprehension off her face and out of her voice. "Why was that?"

"My work assignment was to clean and inspect the furnaces, the old one in Fox Hall and the newer one in Penington Place. But the one in Fox needed a whole lot of work. I had to go out and pick up replacement parts, so it was nearly nine before I got finished. It didn't feel right to claim overtime for work I should have finished on my shift, so I clocked out at 9:00, went to Subway for supper, then headed straight to Penn."

"Do you know what time that was?" *Remember you're not a policewoman from Scotland Yard, Ruthalice Michels, you're a pastor.*

"Probably close to ten. I know I spent a good hour and a half in Penn because it was just after midnight when I got home." A melancholy smile settled briefly on his lips. "Nora was still awake listening to hymns on the Christian radio station."

Ira squeezed the fabric of his green work pants between his fingers.

"Ruthalice," he raised his head as a look of agony crept across his face, "I think I'm going to lose my job." His short powerful hands ceased moving. "You see, I started the fire."

Ruthalice seesawed between curiosity and disbelief, her stomach churning. "How could you have started the fire, Ira?" she asked, ignoring his first comment. "It began in the newspaper in the cubbyhole. That's nowhere near the furnace."

Ira crossed his ankles and tucked his feet under the orange chair. "I went to confession yesterday, Ruthalice, because I have fallen back into the sinful habit of smoking cigarettes again." He lifted his right hand and waved off the empathy he sensed rising to Ruthalice's lips. "I smoked while I worked on the furnace," he stated simply. "I was afraid security might catch me if I left the building with a cigarette in my mouth, so I tossed the butt into that recess halfway up the stairs. I thought it was empty." His eyes began to fill with tears. "So that is why I am the one responsible for the fire."

"I want us to pray together, Ira," she said. "Is that all right with you?"

"I'd like that very much." He interlocked his fingers and bowed his head.

Ruthalice finished her prayer with words from the Twenty-third Psalm. "Even though I walk through the valley of death, I will fear no evil because you, oh Lord, are with me, your rod and your staff they comfort me. Amen."

Ira crossed himself, then kissed his fingertips. "God has forgiven my weakness for smoking. Now I must accept the consequences of my carelessness." He looked at the campus minister without a trace of fear. "Will you come with me to the President's office, Ruthalice?"

"Of course, I will Ira. When do you want to talk with Richard?"

"Now." He blushed. "If possible. I want to get this off my conscience."

Ruthalice spoke briefly with Lynn and hung up the phone. "Richard's out of town for the rest of the day, but we have an appointment tomorrow morning at 9:15."

"I will be there."

Ruthalice stood in the doorway and watched the sturdy little man shuffle down the long narrow hallway. She waved goodbye as the outer door swung shut behind him.

"God bless you and keep you, Ira Tibbett. May your courage and resolve be strong when you speak your truth tomorrow morning." She moved back into her office. "And dear Lord, please guide Richard into a place of wisdom, compassion, and forgiveness."

## CHAPTER TWENTY-NINE

"You're awfully quiet this morning." Cliff leaned against the kitchen sink as the fresh morning sunshine streamed across the linoleum floor. Dozens of dust bunnies appeared out of nowhere.

"Ira Tibbetts started the fire," Ruthalice said as she closed the refrigerator door. "He came to tell me he was in the basement Tuesday night servicing the furnace for the winter." She joined Cliff at the kitchen window and slipped her hands into his. "He told me yesterday that he tossed a lighted cigarette butt into the cubbyhole on his way up the stairs. He made an appointment with Richard this morning." Ruthalice touched the frost-covered window glass and traced a circle with her fingertip. "He's asked me to go with him."

"Our mystery smoker. What else starts a fire," he said tenderly, "beside lightning or a short?"

Ruthalice watched a red-bellied woodpecker work its way tail-first down the tree trunk, poking its beak into the rough surface as it hunted for bugs.

"He's going to be let go, Cliff. Richard will have no other choice." The woodpecker flew away chattering noisily. "Not only did Ira violate the no-smoking on campus ordinance, but apparently this isn't the first time he's misrepresented himself on the time sheet."

"And—" the words stuck in his throat.

"And what, Cliff?" Ruthalice looked up in alarm. "What are you thinking?"

"It's conceivable he committed a crime. I just hope to God Tibbetts is not charged with arson."

"But Ira didn't know the cubbyhole was stuffed with combustibles. He's just as much a victim of this awful fire as Gideon is." Even as she protested, Ruthalice felt the utter futility of doing so. "It's the fire marshal who makes the arson call, right, not the college?" She suddenly felt queasy.

"Correct."

Reading each other's mind, they turned and began rinsing the dishes, grateful for at least one activity over which they had some control. Cliff accepted the plates from Ruthalice's wet hands and placed them on the bottom rack of the dishwasher.

"Richard will be reasonable in his decision regarding Ira, but Angus—" Cliff's voice trailed off.

"—will be fit to be tied," Ruthalice added, resigned to the fact the director of facilities carried around a short fuse, which seemed to easily ignite more often than not. "This has all the makings of a no-good, rotten, lousy, very bad day," Ruthalice announced. "I'm going to need a first-class attitude adjustment before taking on Suzy Henson's Daughters at four-thirty."

Lost in his own thoughts, Clifford placed the black-and-white cow pitcher in the dishwasher and raised the door with his foot.

"Do you know how old Ira is?"

"I'd guess mid-sixties, but it's only a guess. Both of their girls are grown, and I know they have at least one grandson."

By unspoken agreement the M&Ms stopped talking. They'd done as much as they could for the time being. Cliff grabbed his leather satchel off the boot box in the mudroom as Ruthalice lifted her woolen shawl from its peg inside the kitchen door.

"I'm probably going to be late tonight, Sweetheart," she said, following Cliff into the garage. "Weeks ago, I let Suzy rope me into speaking to her Daughters of Sarah group at four-thirty. She made a shameless appeal to my vanity by informing me she'd already told her group that my take on the wives of David is the best she'd ever heard by anyone, anytime, anyplace." Ruthalice rolled her eyes in mock horror. "By the time Suzy serves high tea and the ladies do their round-the-horn 'what's your favorite woman in the Bible' introductions, it will be well after five before I get my fifteen minutes of fame."

"Oh, the sacrifices you pastors have to endure." Cliff swung open the door to his truck and tossed his briefcase onto the seat. "Makes me glad I'm a simple malacologist stuck at a little denominational college in the middle of southwest Ohio who gets to indulge his passion for clams and mussels by teaching invertebrate zoology once every other year."

Ruthalice grinned and batted her eyelashes. "Not a bad price to pay for being able to stay put on your family farm with an adoring wife thrown in to sweeten the deal."

He swung himself into the truck, chuckling. "On a more practical note, is this a head's up that I'm probably the one making supper tonight?"

"If you want to eat before eight o'clock, it is." She stood between the vehicles. "I'll see you this evening, Sweetheart," she said as they exchanged a perfunctory goodbye kiss through the open truck window.

Ruthalice climbed into her car, backed out of the garage, and sat at the top of the driveway until Cliff turned onto Fair Ridge Road. She collected her thoughts, closing with her daily morning prayer. "May I serve your purposes in everything I say and do today and every day. Please show me how. Thank you. Amen."

Ira knocked on the half-open door at five-past-nine dressed in a brand new, Kelly-plaid flannel shirt, tucked snuggly into nearly new, navy blue work pants. A black belt held everything securely in place.

"May we pray before going over to Fox Hall?" he asked.

Ruthalice took his calloused hands in hers as they bowed their heads. Ira let go of her hands and crossed himself when she had finished.

"Thank you, Ruthalice. I'm ready now."

Neither one spoke as they crossed the parking lot and climbed the stairs to President Willson's corner office. Richard looked up from his desk and spotted them standing side by side in the outer office.

"Come in, Ruthalice, Ira. I'll be with you shortly."

Ira waited until Ruthalice chose a seat, then sat down to her left. The president laid his fountain pen on top of the yellow pad, closed the office door, and joined the circle.

"What is it you wish to talk with me about?" he asked kindly, skipping the perfunctory opening chit-chat. "I understand this has something to do with the recent fire in Penington Place." Richard focused his complete attention on Ira, prepared to hear whatever the old handyman had to say.

Twenty minutes later, Ira followed his campus minister down the stairs and back across the parking lot to Frame Meetinghouse. Without speaking they entered the worship room at the far end of the building and sat side by side on the first bench inside the door.

"It could have been worse," Ira began, rubbing both palms on his thighs. "With six months' severance pay and Social Security starting on my birthday in April, plus Nora's disability payments, we can make it OK." He glanced sideways at Ruthalice. "It was awful nice having someone else in the room. Thank you for coming with me," he added shyly, a thin smile playing at the corner of his lips.

"I am grateful you confided in me, Ira." She returned his smile. "Is there anything else I can do to be supportive of you and Nora at this time?

"Could you come by and visit her, maybe later this week?"

"Of course," Ruthalice replied immediately.

"Continue to pray for us."

"I will hold both you and Nora in the Light of Christ."

Ira leaned forward, squeezed the edge of the bench and pushed himself to his feet. "I'll go empty my locker now."

Ruthalice rose to stand beside him and extended her right hand. "You have been a good and faithful member of the Emerick College maintenance team all these years." She swallowed the lump in her throat. "Go in God's peace, Ira Tibbetts. I only wish you were leaving under different circumstances."

"Me too." He inhaled deeply, then forced his breath out with a whoosh, as if to expel all evil spirits that might linger inside. "I will meet with the police this afternoon and fill out a written affidavit." His voice quivered and dropped to a whisper. "With God's help, Nora and I will walk through this dark valley as we have done so many times before."

As Ira headed for the maintenance building and his personal locker for the last time, Ruthalice sank onto the padded bench.

"Thank you, God; thank you, Richard; thank you, Angus, for all your compassion and care under these emotionally charged circumstances," she whispered.

Ruthalice heard the gentle swish as the meeting room door slid over the carpet and glanced over her right shoulder to see who had entered. Barbara Carroll quickly scanned the room, spotted Ruthalice, and walked over. The dean of students smoothed her beige corduroy skirt over her elegant legs and gracefully sat down.

"I was on my way to the library and thought I might find you in here."

"Word travels fast."

"I got Richard's email at nine-thirty. Apparently, he notified President's Council members the minute you two walked out the door." She paused. "We've been requested to keep this confidential until Angus informs the rest of the maintenance crew."

Barbara fixed her gaze on the back of the bench directly in front of them. She rubbed its smooth surface with both hands, then turned to Ruthalice. "How is Ira taking his dismissal?"

"Pretty philosophically actually. I don't know Nora very well, but she's always struck me as a woman who has suffered so much in her lifetime, she will absorb this as just one more burden to be borne." Ruthalice rubbed the crease in her forehead with her middle finger. "They are people of strong faith. When he was in my office yesterday, he told me it was Nora who urged him to go to confession Sunday morning, even though he hadn't told her the whole story. 'She can see into my soul,' he said."

"Ira's lucky to have such support," Barbara said wistfully. "Something like this would have been Steve's excuse to get the hell out of Dodge. Through sickness was never part of the marriage vows he intended to honor."

Ruthalice remained silent, allowing the twinge of regret over her own minimal support of the Carrolls during their tumultuous divorce to run its course.

"Well, enough of the pity party." The dean's hands dropped to her lap. "I came by to tell you something interesting, Ruthalice. Evelyn stopped by my office a few minutes ago and informed me that one of the students on the clean-up crew found a flip-flop in the basement of Penn Place."

Ruthalice jerked to attention. "Really? Where was it?"

"Angus had a work crew in there Sunday afternoon, and one of the kids found it in the corner of the coal bin. I didn't even know there was a coal bin in the basement, did you?" With no response forthcoming, Barbara continued her story. "Anyway, Richard informed the police who showed up shortly thereafter to collect this new piece of evidence, but now that Ira's confessed to starting the fire, I'm not sure what an errant flip-flop has to do with the price of cheese." Barbara chuckled and shook her head. "Surely our dear old Ira didn't clean the furnace in flip-flops, leaving one behind as he scampered up the stairs."

Ruthalice interlaced her fingers, slid her arms between her knees and leaned forward deep in thought. Barbara gently placed a hand on her colleague's back.

"What's troubling you, Ruthalice?"

"Something just occurred to me, Babs, that's all. I need time to cogitate a bit longer, if you don't mind."

Taking the hint, Barbara rose to her feet. "Of course." She stopped at the door. "Oh, there is one more thing, Ruthalice. When I called my RAs together last Friday night, I asked if they knew of any student celebrations planned for this fall. I was thinking somebody might have snuck fireworks in for something like that."

"Good thinking, Babs. No wonder you're such an excellent dean of students."

"Be that as it may, the students told me the Delta Omega sorority is celebrating its fiftieth anniversary on campus on the twenty-ninth of October. They were also quite certain that if the men's soccer team manages to win the divisional championship, there will be a 'freaking awesome bonfire.'" She grinned. "Their words, not mine."

"That's Priscilla Brinkley's sorority, isn't it?"

"I believe so," the dean replied. She allowed the door to close of its own weight behind her.

## CHAPTER THIRTY

Ruthalice crossed the room and stood in front of
the tall, narrow, meetinghouse windows. Outside on the sidewalk, four male students, gym
bags slung over their shoulders, playfully shoved each
other as they sauntered to the athletic facility. Ruthalice watched them pass and felt a surge of energy.

"It's time to find Charles," she said, suddenly clear
about what to do next. "He's going to hear about the
flip-flop any minute now, and I want to be the one to
tell him."

She took the stairs inside Fox Hall as fast as she
could and was gasping for breath by the time she arrived
at Charles' second floor office. The class schedule was
taped to the door: History Seminar, T/Th 10–11:30 a.m.

She scowled at her watch. "That's another forty-five
minutes before he's finished." *Now what, Sherlock?*
Ruthalice walked to the copy room and found a discarded pad of sticky notes beside the paper clips. She tore
off the top square and, using the only pencil she could
locate, wrote: "Call me ASAP, RaM" and stuck the note
to Charles' office door. *That's the best you can do for now,
kiddo, unless you're planning to barge into class.*

"If I can't reach Charles without interrupting the
seminar, then neither can anyone else," she said and
headed back to her office.

By two-ten, Ruthalice was unable to stand it any
longer. "OK, Professor Charles E. Hopkins, I've tried
unsuccessfully to get hold of you at least three times

since your class ended. It's time to take matters into my own hands and storm the Citadel."

Ruthalice ascended the stairs to the second floor of Fox Hall one more time and pounded on the wooden door. She rattled the doorknob in the vain hope she might loosen the latch enough to break in and discover her old friend asleep at his desk. When that didn't work, she had no choice but to head back to her office.

Still hoping Charles would call, Ruthalice waited as long as she dared before finally heading to the white colonial home of Suzanne Matilda Polk Henson and her Daughters of Sarah gathering. Bible in hand, Ruthalice lifted the brass fleur-de-lys door knocker and let it drop. Enormous ceramic pots full of mums of every color known to humankind were artfully scattered across the spacious front porch. Water gurgled as it descended through a fountain of clay pots, adding its contribution to the scene of comfortable hospitality. Standing there, Ruthalice was filled with joy. *Everything seems to be saying: WELCOME!*

"My goodness, Ruthalice Michels, don't just stand there," Suzy exclaimed, sweeping her into the brownie-scented interior. "Girls, girls, our speaker's here. Come and say hello."

With a bright smile plastered on her face, Ruthalice accepted the rose-covered teacup and joined eight women clustered around a flower-bedecked dining room table. *Only ninety minutes to go, girl. You can do this.* The group took their seats and spent the next thirty minutes introducing themselves.

When it was finally Ruthalice's turn, she led the octet of elderly Daughters back to the royal court of King David and his many wives, losing track of both the time and the jumble of conflicting concerns she carried with her since the fire.

"OK, girls, we've got time for one more question." Suzy nodded at the tiny woman across the room gently waving a pale, white hand.

"Yes, Mrs. Crimp," Ruthalice replied as the woman shrunk back into her seat, "you're absolutely right. I do make the argument that Abigail is the earliest woman pacifist on record. She wisely headed off a disastrous confrontation between Nabal, her drunken husband, and David, the hot-headed young shepherd whose hospitality and protection her spouse had just insulted. As a result, David took Abigail as his wife after, as you so delicately phrased it, her nasty old husband Nabal was struck dead by the Lord."

"Let's give Ruthalice a nice round of appreciation, shall we?" Suzy led the applause, then reached under her chair and extracted a large box wrapped in gold leaf paper with a matching bow stuck to the lid. Suzy beamed around the circle of perfumed seniors dressed in their casual best and placed the feather-light package in Ruthalice's hands. "A little thank you from the Daughters of Sarah circle."

Ruthalice slipped her fingers under the tape at each end and lifted the lid. Inside lay an exquisitely delicate turquoise and silver globe. As Ruthalice lifted it from the pale, yellow tissue, light seemed to burst forth from the middle of the sphere. Fascinated by the changing patterns dancing inside, Ruthalice turned to her hostess.

"Where on earth did you find such a gorgeous thing?"

"You can thank Martha Jean," Suzy said, indicating the blue-haired lady to Ruthalice's left. "She bought it on their recent trip to Venice."

"Gerald and I went to the glassblowers the last day of our tour." Martha Jean patted the back of Ruthalice's right hand with her plump fingers. "Let me tell you, it was not cheap, so I'm glad you like it." She smoothed the linen skirt over her thighs. "I bought a bright red one for myself. Truthfully though," she began, her voice now loud enough for everyone in the room to hear, "I never cared for that shade of blue, so when Suzanne asked me about a—"

"OK, girls," Suzy said, quickly breaking in, "don't forget we meet at Jenny Feingold's next month, same time, different station."

Twenty minutes later Suzy said goodbye to the last Daughter and reappeared in the living room.

"You'll have to forgive Martha Jean, my dear," she said, handing Ruthalice her shawl. "She's a bit scatter-brained these days, I'm afraid. Half the time she doesn't think about what she's saying. It's a shame really. Martha Jean Perkins used to be Oakes Quarry's 'hostess with the most-est,' but I'm afraid those days are long gone."

"Good heavens, Suzy, don't worry about it," Ruthalice assured her warmly. "The ornament is truly gorgeous. I'm going to hang it front and center on our Christmas tree."

"Oh good, that makes me feel better. Did you see the shepherd and his two lambs inside?" Grinning at Ruthalice's perplexed look, Susy Henson gave a husky chuckle. "I didn't think so. Well, look more closely when you get home." She stepped onto the hand-knotted, navy blue welcome mat to stand beside Ruthalice. "Take my word for it, my dear. There is a young shepherd inside, I promise."

Ruthalice had just started across the front porch, carefully cradling the box with its delicate contents against her chest, when Suzy tapped her on the shoulder. *Every time you stop me like this, you get all conspiratorial and try to involve me in something I don't want any part of.*

"OK, Ruthalice Michels, now that our busybody friends have gone home, I want the complete scoop on the recent incident on campus." She fixed Ruthalice with the LOOK, the one that always sent a rash of goose bumps along Ruthalice's arms when she was a kid.

"The complete scoop on which incident, exactly?" Ruthalice replied, opting to play the dumb card, knowing full well it never worked.

"On the conflagration in Penington Place, of course. Isn't the campus minister privy to all the secrets, dirty or otherwise?"

"Good grief, Suzy," Ruthalice retorted, suddenly annoyed by the blatant attempt to pry information, confidential or otherwise, out of her. *Annoyance is a more mature response to Suzy's badgering than your other choice which is panic.* "Just read the Boone County paper, and you'll know as much as I do."

"You are stonewalling me, Ms. Michels, just like your mother used to do when I got too close to the truth." Suzy glowered at the nearest pot of mums and severed two dead heads from their stems with a pinch of forefinger and thumb. "Even as a teenager, you never were much good when it came to gossip." She tossed the shriveled-up blossoms over the porch rail. "What a meddling pain in the you-know-what I must have been."

Ruthalice was about to offer a limp version of you-weren't-that-bad when Suzy abruptly changed the subject.

"Thank you so much for coming this afternoon, Ruthalice. I know you have many more important things to do with your time and talent than sit around doing a Bible study with a group of little old ladies."

"And miss being the recipient of this stunningly beautiful ornament? No way, Jose." Ruthalice leaned over and planted a kiss on Suzy's left cheek and squeezed her shoulder. Suzy reached up and caught Ruthalice's hand.

"There is tragedy surrounding this fire," Suzy said softly. "I can feel it in my bones."

Ruthalice picked her way around globs of soggy leaves strewn about on the sidewalk by an unseen hand and slipped into the car. She laid her present on the front seat and turned the ignition. *Just when I've given up on her, Suzy manages to come through with a surprising bit of insight.* As she gazed at the white colonial home, a light came on and drove the encroaching darkness off the front porch. *What would Suzy do if Gideon were suddenly dropped in her lap?* Startled by the query's clarity, Ruthalice closed her eyes.

"I honestly don't know," she whispered to the inner voice, "but I'm having a tough time picturing Suzy Henson slamming the door in Gideon's face and leaving him stranded on the front porch, whether he's a refugee or an undocumented worker or a little green man from Mars."

Ruthalice turned the ignition and smiled. "You would bring Gideon into your home just as you did me when I was a lost little girl and, if you had second thoughts? Well, you'd find a way to deal with them afterwards."

## CHAPTER THIRTY-ONE

The gentle niggling Ruthalice recognized as God's persistent tug at the edges of her heart remained with her all the way home. "All right, Lord," she said, shutting off the car engine. "I'm open and I'm listening."

The skittish miscellaneous thoughts in her brain fell into place like jumbled jigsaw pieces, creating a complete picture. "Oh my gosh," she cried leaping out of the car. "Why didn't I see that before?"

She dropped her bag on the cluttered countertop, flung her shawl on the breakfast nook table, and ran into the living room.

"Cliff!" She threw herself onto the couch and tugged at his sleeve like a spoiled child. "Listen to this!"

He lowered the *Boone County Gazette* and stared at her.

"You've discovered the formula for lasting world peace? Anything less can't possible merit this much enthusiasm." He folded the paper and laid his hands in his lap. "Tell me what's gotten you so revved up."

"I've figured out who put the fireworks in the basement." Cliff's right eyebrow shot up. "Babs came into the meeting room this morning after Ira left. The long and short of our conversation is the Delts have been planning all semester to celebrate their fiftieth anniversary on campus at the end of October." She leaned forward. "Now, the last time Rani Brown was in my office she told me that when she got up around one fifteen Wednesday morning, she looked out the dorm window and saw somebody running from behind Penington Place."

"But that was Gideon." He turned toward her and rested his right arm on the back of the couch.

"That's my hunch as well, Cliff, but think about this. Rani overheard the girls bragging about how spectacular their little caper would be. I've been a bit slow on the uptake here, but I think I've finally put two and two together." Ruthalice stood up and began to pace back and forth in front of the sofa.

"I know Priscilla works upstairs in the Archives because I saw her nameplate on the student worker's desk. Ernestine wouldn't keep track of her comings and goings because she belongs up there, even though she doesn't work in the Alumni office."

"Invisible and in plain sight."

"I couldn't have said it better, my dear Watson, and I know Priscilla Brinkley is a Delt," she said, sitting down beside him.

"Let me ask you something before we go any further with this." He put his hand on her knee. "Has anything more come of those two men Springer saw hanging around the night of the fire?"

"I stopped in for coffee yesterday and Missy did mention something about them, but it wasn't definitive. She wanted me to know she told the cops that one was a man, but the other person was a woman. Missy is basing her opinion on their body shape and watching how they interacted." Ruthalice shrugged. "Whatever. And for what it's worth, she's also convinced the male figure had a cast on his hand."

"As far as I'm aware, the only kid on campus wearing a cast on his hand is Ted Cope," Cliff said helpfully.

"Priscilla and Theodore?" The M&Ms stared at each other. Cliff blinked first.

"I don't suppose there's anything which says they can't be an item," he said.

"Now there's a sobering thought. The Explosive Duo: Perpetually Peeved Priscilla paired with Tempestuous Theatrical Theodore." Ruthalice shuddered. "It boggles the mind."

Cliff scratched the top of his head. "Let's revisit your hypothesis: Priscilla has a motive for purchasing fireworks and the means to ensure their existence is kept secret."

Ruthalice shifted uncomfortably. "I don't know that I'm ready to accuse Priscilla of blowing up Penington Place and hauling her into court." She reached for Cliff's hand and gripped it tightly.

"She could be an accessory to a crime."

Ruthalice traced the knuckles of their intertwined fingers then let her right hand settle lightly on top.

"I think you're close, Sweetheart." Cliff added his left hand to the pile in her lap. The warmth and weight felt reassuring. She smiled and leaned her head against his shoulder.

# CHAPTER THIRTY-TWO

The next morning Ruthalice set the class notes on her desk, draped the worsted shawl over her shoulders, and headed for Fox. The heavy clouds had finally moved off to the east, allowing the sun to resume its rightful place in the late October sky. The birds seemed to have come out of hiding as well, now that the rain had ceased.

Ruthalice climbed the stairs and stopped outside Charles' office door. A gruff "present" greeted her knock. As she entered the spacious office, Charles raised his head, smiled weakly, and motioned her to the single empty chair.

"Hallo, Ruthalice." She closed the door and sat down. "Looks like an official visit from our campus minister."

"Charles, there's been a new development," Ruthalice began, feeling like the specter of death standing at the parlor door. "Maintenance found a flip-flop in the basement of Penington Place."

"Am I to assume that is why you left numerous messages to call you yesterday afternoon?" Ruthalice nodded. "The hounds are closing in," he intoned, "thus urgency is required on my part to resolve this unfortunate matter." Charles leaned his upper body against the edge of the desk and stared across the cluttered surface between them.

"It belongs to Gideon, doesn't it, Charles?"

The senior member of Emerick's faculty looked around the office, his eyes passing slowly along rows of beloved texts and biographies lined up for inspection.

"I've got over two hundred and fifty volumes in this room and an additional fifty-plus in my library at home." He articulated each word in his cultured British accent, a habit he fell into when deeply troubled. "Gideon told me Sunday he was unable to find his other flip-flop." His eyes rested on a small, pale gray, soapstone carving of an Inuit hunter, spear in hand. "Foolishly I dismissed it as a trivial point, pointing out that it was too bloody cold to wear sandals anyway and promising we'd stop at Wally and purchase proper footgear on our way to your home."

Charles gritted his teeth.

"Gideon snuck out last night to go to work for God's sake." The words spewed out in a torrent of pent-up frustration. "You know what he said to me when I chewed him out? 'I give my word to Miss Green. She count on me, Professor Curly. I must go to my job.' Bugger it all!"

"God love him," Ruthalice said, her voice thick with emotion. "Just think, Charles, how good Gideon must feel knowing someone is counting on him, that he's needed somewhere."

"That's as it may be, but I feel like a damn green-horn rookie cowboy trying to rein in a young stallion!" The old professor shook his head. "First the lantern, then Gideon sneaks off to the warehouse, and now the flip-flop!" He fixed her with a grim stare. "By now our esteemed president will have informed the chief of police, and we will be overrun by a fleet of inspectors combing the campus for clues as to its ownership."

Half hidden beneath bushy black brows, the professor's eyes hardened along with his voice. "He may have managed his initial scamper without being spotted, but our young friend will soon be flushed from his den like a fox."

Charles grasped his jacket lapels with both hands and pulled on his coat until the collar stretched tightly across the back of his neck. "I'm not cut out for this, Ruthalice," he said, his voice heavy with exhaustion. "I want to be done with this damnable interruption and the burden fate has dropped upon me." He stuffed his hands into the pockets of his trousers and leaned back in his chair.

"There was this old soldier who kept babbling about mustard gas in the First War, how it burned and poisoned everything. What if the Germans use it again? What if I fall on the third rail of the train track and get electrocuted like my pa said I would if I wasn't careful? He went on and on like that, night after night scaring the holy blazes out of me." Charles raised his head. "After hiding from the Blitzkrieg in the Underground, I was terrified of everything, Ruthalice: the dark, the shadows, the unseen, creepy-crawlies."

"In spite of your fear you carry on." Ruthalice met his gaze with a warm smile, "Like the trusted compatriot and friend you are."

"Yes, well."

Ruthalice watched as he laid his hands on the desk, one on top of the other, seemingly lost in a time warp of his own creation. Then without warning, the old professor straightened up and squared his shoulders.

"It is the brain, the little gray cells on which one must rely," he began, slipping into an affected Belgian accent. "Yes, Miss Lemon, the hounds have caught the scent, but that kind of business does not succeed against Hercule Poirot!"

His laugh startled and alarmed her.

*Dear God, we need your wisdom and courage here real fast.* Ruthalice stood up and walked around the desk. *And please keep the hounds away from Gideon and Charles,* she added for good measure.

"Cliff and I will do all we can, Charles," she said, laying a hand on his shoulder, "and please be assured we've told no one about Gideon."

"It never occurred to me that you would." He stiffened. "However, my dear Ruthalice, the noose is tightening; constables are on the prowl." Charles got to his feet and without so much as a "fare thee well," walked out of the room.

Ruthalice waited while two faculty members walked by. She pulled the office door closed behind her, and hurried down the stairs. *I've no idea what Charles is planning to do, but it's time I acted on my hunch about Priscilla Brinkley.*

## CHAPTER THIRTY-THREE

Ruthalice slipped through the Jones Student Center lobby, swarming with students, and into the dean's outer office. Barbara Carroll finished her phone conversation, and waved Ruthalice on in.

"Can I get you a cup?" she asked, brandishing her gold-trimmed white mug. "I need another shot before lunch."

"No, thanks, Babs, I'm floating as it is."

Barbara Francelia Carroll was head and shoulders above the rest of her colleagues in the "got class" department. Intricate lattice teak bookends supported a handful of colorfully bound books. Exquisitely framed reproductions of Van Gogh's *Starry Night* and a Turner seascape balanced each other perfectly on opposite walls. Four handsome chairs upholstered in a pinstriped pearl-and-peach fabric created a square on the octagonal Persian rug, which covered nearly every square inch of floor from desk to outer wall.

Ruthalice remained standing in the doorway. "Every time I come over here, Babs, I feel like I should check my shoes for doggie doodoo or my skirt for cookie crumbs before setting foot in your office." She swept her hands down over her stomach. *However,* she reminded herself, *you can't tell a book by its cover. I defy anyone to find a more perceptive and refreshingly straightforward dean of students.*

"So, business or pleasure?" Barbara sat down in the chair closest to her desk and nodded toward a matching seat for Ruthalice.

"You said the Delts have an anniversary coming up. I'm wondering if one of the sorority sisters decided firecrackers would add a little pizzazz to their celebration."

Barbara stared thoughtfully into her cup.

"Isn't Priscilla Brinkley a Delt?"

"Yes, president actually." The dean raised her head. "She and Jen Blake, her roommate, live in Douglas Hall, but spend a good deal of time at the chapter house on Mulligan Avenue."

"She is the student worker in the Quaker Archives." Ruthalice rested her elbows on the cushioned armrest. "What's your professional take on Priscilla?"

The dean of students picked a minuscule piece of lint off the left sleeve of her jacket.

"A bit of a challenge. Priscilla is listed as a sophomore, but Emerick is the third college she's attended in as many years, having flunked out of the first and despising the second." Barbara placed her hands fingertip to fingertip and raised them to her lips. "Papa Brinkley's paying the full ride and appears to be generous with his financial support, but the occasional Saks Fifth Avenue birthday present is the extent of his parental involvement. I've arrived at this conclusion from comments overheard here and there," she added dryly.

Ruthalice nodded. "Out of sight, out of mind."

The dean squeezed her upper lip between her forefingers then let her hands drop into her lap. "There's a bit of the devil-take-the-hindmost about her. I am aware that the first floor RA has tangled with Priscilla on more than one occasion."

"My way or the highway?"

"My way or just try and stop me." Barbara turned in order to face the campus minister. "Her dad's a big wig CEO who apparently is on the road more than he's home. He came to campus for Parent's Day, which earned him a few brownie points in my book. Priscilla's mother is a stay-at-home housewife who lives virtually alone in their beachfront condo on the Outer Banks. According to her daughter, Mother does a lot of squabbling with her neighbors."

"The Brinkleys sent their daughter an awfully long way from home for her third attempt at college," Ruthalice replied. "But at least they're not 'helicopter parents,' ready to swoop down at the first sign of offspring angst." Ruthalice looked puzzled. "Does make me wonder though how they heard about Emerick. We're not exactly on the radar screen for the North Carolina surf and sun crowd."

"An acquaintance of her mother's brother has a daughter who attended Emerick six years ago and loved it," Barbara said, a hint of amusement in her voice. Her tone changed as she glanced at her wristwatch. "Anything else on your mind today, Ruthalice?" she asked. "I've got an engagement at noon."

"Nope, but this has been extremely helpful, Babs. Thanks." Ruthalice got to her feet. "I'm working on a hunch."

"Please keep me in the loop," the dean replied, then added almost as an afterthought, "Firecrackers would make for a rather spectacular fiftieth anniversary party. They are illegal by the way."

"So I'm told."

Ruthalice headed back downstairs and stepped back into the sunshine. Thinking an unannounced pastoral visit from the campus minister might just jar something loose, she headed straight for Penington Place.

Upstairs, a hand-lettered sign hung around the neck of a handsome iron horse statue on the student worker's desk. "B back at 2" was penciled in bold script.

*Phooey! Well, that settles that. It's on to Plan B, and I do believe Plan B begins with lunch.*

## CHAPTER THIRTY-FOUR

R uthalice was back at Penn Place at 2:15. Despite the open windows, the smell of smoke hovered in the open area at the top of the stairs. Ruthalice spotted Priscilla sitting at the small student desk along the west wall, casually flipping through a magazine. She headed across the archival space, skirting the boxes of books and file folders occupying the middle of the room.

"You've got quite a view of Dalton Hall across campus from up here, Priscilla," Ruthalice said. "I'll bet this is a lovely place to work."

"It's OK." The smile was non-committal. "We're not officially open right now." She ran her fingers through silky, shoulder-length, blue-black hair. "I'm just taking a break from the packing." The young woman folded the corner of the page and closed the magazine. She fixed her visitor with a sanguine smile.

Knowing she was about to go head-to-head with a real pro, Ruthalice favored her adversary with a sweet smile. "You a horse lover?" she asked. She lay her right hand on the iron horse head and ran her fingers between the cold metal ears.

"Have been all my life." Priscilla's eyes lit up. "I've got my dapple-gray mare, Marie Antoinette, boarded out at Candlewood Farm."

"Nice," Ruthalice nodded approvingly. "Get much opportunity to ride her?"

"Couple times a week and for sure on the weekends." Priscilla glanced at her *Western Horsewoman,* turning the magazine so the cover lined up with the edge of the desk. "Dad took pity on me being stuck on campus every weekend and had her hauled up here from North Carolina." Her gaze wandered to the window. "Sure beats sitting around the dorm."

"I've heard that social life on campus leaves something to be desired on the weekends."

"It sucks." Priscilla dug an iPhone out of her designer jeans pocket and peered at the screen. She gave a bored shrug of her shoulders and laid the phone on top of her magazine. "Did you need something in the archives?"

"No, not really, I just came by to chat." Ruthalice crossed her arms. "I understand the Delta Omega sorority is celebrating its fiftieth anniversary in a few weeks."

Priscilla got to her feet and shoved a cardboard box into position with her foot. She bent over and began stuffing well-worn leather and clothbound volumes into the empty carton. It was all Ruthalice could do to keep herself from snatching these lovely new orphans out of the young woman's uncaring hands and placing them properly into their temporary home herself, thus affording them the respect they deserved.

"Got anything special planned?" she asked instead, opting to maintain the tone of curious and friendly campus minister.

"Oh, the usual stuff." The young woman made an elaborate point of stifling a yawn. "Why do you ask?"

Given the opening she needed, Ruthalice charged through. "The fire marshal determined the fire was started by a cigarette tossed into that recess in the wall halfway down the basement stairs." Priscilla's hands hovered over the box by her feet. "Somebody took the time to crumble up newspapers and then stuff them in front of an old cardboard box."

"Why would anybody do that?"

"To disguise the fact there were fireworks in the box."

Priscilla raised both shoulders in an elaborate shrug and turned to face Ruthalice. "And why are you telling me all this?"

"Just wondering what you make of my little theory."

"And what theory would that be?"

"That fireworks would make a spectacular addition to the fiftieth anniversary celebration."

"Listen, I'm president and in charge of the whole celebration thing, so I would totally know if any of the sorority sisters are thinking about pulling a stunt like that."

"Then you don't mind asking around, right Priscilla? Especially since it's a first-degree misdemeanor in this state to possess fireworks, let alone discharge them."

Ruthalice picked up the worn leather-bound copy of John Woolman's *Journal* patiently waiting to be packed, then laid it on top of the stack in the cardboard box. "The fine for first-time offenders could run as high as a thousand dollars with a possible jail time of six months," she added casually, watching for a reaction out of the corner of her eye.

*Boy you're good, or innocent.* "Can you imagine either the chief of police or President Willson turning a blind eye to a flagrantly illegal fireworks display?" Ruthalice tapped the desktop with her knuckles and turned to leave. "I know I can't."

## CHAPTER THIRTY-FIVE

Moving quickly to the window, Priscilla watched Ruthalice stride across the leaf-strewn lawn toward Frame Meetinghouse. Without a word she snatched the crimson leather shoulder bag her mother picked up at Coach as a going-back-to-college present and headed for the ladies' room. She locked the door behind her and stared at her reflection in the mirror.

"Geesh, I look like a deer caught in the headlights," she moaned, gripping the sink with both hands. "You can't walk across campus looking scared witless." Hearing the click of approaching heels in the hallway, Priscilla turned both faucets on full blast. "Just a minute, Ernestine," she hollered over the rushing water. "I'm almost done."

"I can wait dear," came the reply, "take your time."

Patricia pressed a wet paper towel to her eyes and took a deep breath, tossed the soggy paper in the basket, and shut off the water. Pasting a look of distress on her face, she slowly opened the door.

"I'm so glad you're here, Ernestine, I'm suddenly feeling really, really sick." Priscilla wrapped both arms around her middle. "Would you be awfully inconvenienced if I went home early?"

"Oh, good heavens no, dear, of course not. You do look pretty peaked," she said, examining Priscilla's pale face. "It's all this smoke, I'm certain of it. You'll feel better after you take a deep breath of fresh air." Ernestine exhaled deeply, a weary look of resignation on her thin face. "I doubt anyone will come in. The place looks deserted with all our first-floor windows boarded up." She nodded in the direction of the gathering space. "We're going to be packing things up for quite a while. You'll have no trouble making up your hours."

As Ernestine pulled the bathroom door behind her, Priscilla sped down the stairs before the older woman could change her mind. "The old bat thinks I'm about to toss my cookies," she snickered as she made a bee-line for Douglas Residence Hall. She ran down the hallway and burst through the door of her room.

"My God, you scared me," Jen shrieked, sitting bolt upright on her bed.

Priscilla locked the door behind her, spun the desk chair so its back faced her roommate's bed, and dropped down straddling the seat. "Jen, we've got to talk." She fixed her roommate with the obstinate look the senior Brinkleys had come to dread.

"I've got a chem exam at eight o'clock tomorrow morning, Prissy. Can't whatever it is wait?"

"Now, Jen. Believe me, this is way more important than any chemistry exam."

Jen sighed and laid *The Principles of Organic Chemistry* face down on the bed beside her.

"Ruthalice Michels knows about the fireworks."

Jennifer Blake opened her mouth to protest, but Priscilla cut her off.

"Just listen to me," she hissed. "The cops figure the Penn fire started because some weak-brained yo-yo tossed a cigarette into the box where we stashed our fireworks. So, duh, of course they exploded."

"Oh, no," Jen wailed, covering her face with both hands.

"For heaven's sake, Jen, get a grip. Our smarty-pants campus minister with her let's-play-detective attitude may think she's got it all figured out, but there's no way in hell she can prove they belong to us."

"How can you be so sure, Prissy?" Jen swiped at her eyes with the back of her hand.

"Think about it for a minute. First, we bought them out of state, remember, and the fire destroyed everything, right, so there can't be anything left but ashes." Priscilla joined her roommate on the bed. "Listen, Jen, as long as we just act like normal people and keep our mouths shut, we've got nothing to worry about."

Jen squirmed uncomfortably, then pressed her back against the pale blue cement block wall.

"My parents are going to kill me if I get kicked out of school for this." She inhaled deeply, then cleared her throat. "Mom didn't want me to pledge in the first place. She said Greek life would be a bad influence on me." Jen drew her knees up to her chest and buried her face in her arms.

Momentarily speechless, Priscilla considered her options. This was not the first time one of her brainstorms had gone awry, leaving her to figure a way out of the ensuing mess. Her roommate lifted her head and gave Priscilla a watery smile.

"I guess I feel better, Prissy. I guess everything's going to work out OK. It's just—"

"It's just what, Jen?"

"It's just I feel awful knowing we're responsible for the fire in Penington."

"We are? How do you figure that? What planet are you on, Jennifer?" Priscilla glowered at her roommate.

"Have you taken up smoking and become incredibly stupid at the same time?"

Jumping up, Priscilla clenched her fists and began to pace.

"Firecrackers don't ignite on their own you know, Miss 'A' in Chemistry. This is not a case of spontaneous combustion." She kicked the dresser on her way by. "There's no way in hell anybody can hang that fire on us. It's the idiot and his burning cigarette. How dumb do you have to be to toss a burning butt into a box of newspapers?"

Priscilla stopped beside the bed. "Listen to me, Jennifer Blake, I'm not going down for this one. It wasn't us who ditched a fag in the basement. Neither one of us smokes, so how is any of this our fault?"

"I guess you're right, as always." Jennifer stared glumly at what remained of the once-bright-orange polish on her toenails. "I guess we're going to find out one way or another who gets the blame."

"Trust me on this one, Jen. if we don't screw it up by getting hyper, this whole thing will blow over by Halloween."

## CHAPTER THIRTY-SIX

R uthalice spent what remained of the afternoon writing her bi-weekly "Friendly Musings" for the student newspaper. Satisfied with her essay on the role rumors play in campus life, Ruthalice interlaced her fingers and stretched both arms above her head. *A quick trip to the potty and I'm outta here!* Her half-hearted search for any remaining dirty mugs to rinse out was interrupted by three raps on the door.

"I'm here," she responded automatically as she examined the Support Your Local PBS Station mug with a layer of cocoa in the bottom that was at least two days old.

"Hi, Ruthalice with an 'i.'" Lieutenant Rosemarie Harris stood squarely in the middle of the doorway. Dressed in her navy-blue police uniform, the lieutenant was all business. "We need to talk, Ruthalice."

"Sounds serious, Rosemarie, I'm all ears."

The officer stepped inside and closed the door. Ruthalice motioned to an empty chair, but her visitor remained standing, hands on hips.

"There was just enough left of the original packaging that I was able to decipher three letters and figure out the name of the fireworks manufacturer." Her no-nonsense black eyes met Ruthalice's. "With the help of my whiz-kid, web-dude son, we traced back to the company in Indiana that sells this brand of fireworks. Not bad for a lousy speller like me." A self-congratulatory smile softened her face. "I played around with the letters UND until I came up with Thunder, googled it, and bingo: Thunder Mountain Fire Works. Their logo is 'Choose Your Pyro-Power.' The owner wasn't real happy to hear about the part his merchandise played in this particular caper."

"Whoa, Rosemarie, I'm impressed. I'm going to make you an honorary member of my Puzzlers Are Us club!"

The lieutenant chuckled. "Do I get a nice shiny plaque to hang on my bedroom wall?"

They remained silent for a moment enjoying the lightness of a growing friendship.

"So where do we go from here?"

The smile disappeared. "That's why I'm here, Ruthalice. Thunder Mountain prides itself on keeping very good sales records."

Twenty minutes later, Lieutenant Rosemarie Harris escorted Priscilla Brinkley and Jennifer Blake to the Oakes Quarry police station in her black-and-white squad car. Ruthalice, who had felt duty bound to be present while the girls were confronted, stood watching the taillights disappear along with the excitement she'd felt earlier in the day, imagining herself alongside the likes of Miss Marple and Jessica-what's-her-name, leaving only sadness in its wake.

*God, please protect these impulsive children of yours as they enter their own valley of darkness. They desperately need your love to sustain and guide them.*

As security lights came to life one by one, Ruthalice crossed the campus green and climbed the stairs to the president's office.

"Lynn, I'm here to have a word with Richard."

At the secretary's nod, she crossed the room and

knocked on the frame of the open door. The president glanced up and motioned her in.

"There's something you should know," Ruthalice said calmly and closed the door behind her. Fifteen minutes later she joined Cliff in the parking lot.

"Want me to drive, Sweetheart? You look exhausted."

Ruthalice handed over the car keys and opened the door on the passenger's side. She tossed her shoulder bag in the back seat and leaned wearily against the headrest.

"In fact," he added as his wife closed her eyes. "How 'bout we eat at Louellen's tonight?"

## CHAPTER THIRTY-SEVEN

"Want to talk?" Cliff asked after the M&Ms had placed their orders.

"Do you want the full scoop or the Reader's Digest expedited version?" she replied, squeezing his hand.

"Whatever you're up for's fine with me. I'm your captive audience up until our food arrives."

"I tested my theory about Priscilla Brinkley and the Delt's fiftieth anniversary. When I pressed her about the idea of setting off fireworks as part of the celebration, she insisted no one was even thinking of such a stunt. Then Lieutenant Harris dropped by the office around four to inform me she was able to track down the manufacturer. After that bit of detective work, it was a piece of cake, apparently. The salesclerk traced the purchase directly to Priscilla Brinkley, credit card and all."

"You're kidding. She used a credit card? What a twisted trail of innocent actions converging into a tangled web of intrigue, resulting in one helluva mess, or something like that." Cliff was suddenly drained of words.

"You know about the flip-flop." Cliff nodded. "Richard told me the cops have it and are holding it as an item of relevance to the investigation." Ruthalice sighed. "I don't know, Cliff, maybe I'm getting a bit paranoid, but Richard gave me a baffled look like he's accusing me of knowing more than I'm letting on."

"I know we're both in this now up to our eyeballs as you are wont to say, Sweetheart, but let's not let our imaginations run away with our combined good sense, OK?" Cliff rubbed his temples. "I spoke with Charles this morning, and he's totally convinced Gideon's about to be flushed out by ICE."

"Charles may be right," she said. "I was doing some looking online this morning and saw a headline that reported forced removals by ICE officials of Somali citizens have more than doubled in the past year." Ruthalice began to weep. *I seem to be doing an inordinate amount of crying these days.*

"Charles may indeed be right, then."

"About being flushed out, yes indeed." Ruthalice fished a wad of Kleenex out of her pocket. "Rosemarie asked me this afternoon if there's another African student on campus."

"Another?" Cliff frowned. "Then she knows about Luther."

"Yes. The 911 dispatcher reported that the caller had a heavy accent that she thought sounded African. Lieutenant Harris located Luther and asked if he'd made the call, and of course he said 'no.'" Ruthalice blew her nose. "Now get this, Cliff, Rosemarie also told me she stopped and questioned an African male in the parking lot of the Warehouse Store who told her he lives on campus. That satisfied her at the time, so she didn't ask his name.'"

"And you said?"

"Luther Mouana is the only African student currently enrolled at Emerick College."

The waiter interrupted their worried looks with two large servings of chicken and dumplings in the richest gravy in town.

After dinner during their shared quiet on the ride home, Ruthalice watched her husband's face flicker as the city lights slipped by. *Like an old silent movie.* He suddenly smiled.

"You know, Ruthalice Michels, for a woman of the cloth, you've become quite the detective, a veritable Rabbi Small in a skirt!"

"Wrong gender and wrong religious tradition," she chuckled, "but I appreciate the flattering comparison."

She leaned over and kissed him on the cheek then rubbed her cold nose against his warm, scratchy face. "Besides the fact Sheppard Place is no longer a safe location for Gideon, the burden of sharing his bachelor pad, day in and day out, is taking its toll on Charles."

"I think you're spot on with that observation, Sweetheart. You know we have a weekly research confab." Ruthalice nodded. "Well, yesterday, Charles said, 'The Bishop of Swithun is relegated to the back seat these days whilst I attend to Gideon's predicament,' which is Charles' way of justifying an entire weekend away from the library and his book research."

Ruthalice watched the internal struggle with the "Gideon affair," as they'd begun calling it, play itself out on his handsome face.

"What are you afraid is going to happen?" he asked as he made the turn into their drive.

"Immigration will swoop in unannounced, deportation papers in hand, and summarily stick Gideon on a plane bound for Somalia. I will never forget witnessing that very thing in the Gatwick Airport outside London. The poor man lay on the floor, hugging his brown paper bag to his chest, pleading with the circle of Bobbies to let him stay in England." She swallowed as she heard the garage door settle with a thud behind them. "There was not a thing I could do. I heard the men in the bar behind me mocking his tears and felt sick to my stomach."

She pulled her heavy braid over her shoulder and rubbed its soft tip against her cheek. "I'm haunted by the image of Gideon, handcuffed to a burly ICE agent, being dragged onto a plane bound for Mogadishu, where he'll be summarily dumped back on the streets."

Cliff gripped the steering wheel with both hands. "My God, the man earned his bachelor's degree fair and square, and look at him now. He's been instructed not to answer the door or telephone; he's relegated to sneaking out three times a week to go to work for a few hours in order to save enough money to somehow get to relatives in the Twin Cities." Cliff turned off the engine then reached up to rub his eyes. "It's exhausting."

"Treat the orphan, the widow, the poor, and the alien among you as one of your own, for you also are sojourners in this land," Ruthalice paraphrased softly. "You know what I think, Cliff? I think our little Emerick College campus right here in Oakes Quarry, Ohio *is* the land upon which you and I and Gideon and Charles and all the rest of us, are sojourning."

By unspoken agreement, the M&Ms left the day's accumulation of papers, notebooks, and other academic paraphernalia on the back seat of the car. Cliff opened the pass-through door to the side yard, and hand-in-hand they crossed the damp lawn to the front porch.

"'The earth is the Lord's and the fullness thereof,'" she recited to the star-filled sky. A great horned owl hooted from the woods. "It's pretty amazing really," she said, leaning her back against the oak rail. "The letters UND on a one-inch scrap of singed cardboard was all Rosemarie had to go on. Her son ran an online search for fireworks manufacturers and found a Thunder Mountain somewhere out west. She was told about their distributor in Richmond, Indiana, and the rest, as they say, is history."

Cliff wrapped his arm around her shoulders and gently guided her through the front door, down the hall, and into the master bedroom. He kicked off his shoes, dropped his jeans on the floor, and slipped between the sheets. "How did the girls react when you confronted them?" he asked, pulling the blanket to his chin.

"Jennifer went ballistic. She collapsed on the bed sobbing, 'I told you they'd find out, Prissy!' It was fairly anticlimactic after that."

"I'll bet." He watched his wife unbraid her hair with her fingers.

"Apparently Priscilla had smuggled the packages into Penn Place several weeks ago and agreed to lock up one afternoon when Ernestine had to leave early. There was nothing suspicious about any of that, so of course Ernestine agreed."

Ruthalice disappeared into the closet and re-emerged in an ankle-length flannel nightie.

"And the motivation for this bit of theater?" Cliff pulled back the covers on her side of the bed.

"To upstage the Gamma's anniversary party last spring. Those two women were obsessed with outdoing the men's fraternity by setting off the most spectacular fireworks show Oakes Quarry had ever seen!"

Ruthalice climbed into bed, pulled the blanket over her shoulder, and propped herself up on her left elbow.

"When Jennifer finally got a grip on herself, her only concern was whether or not the cops had to tell her mother. Lieutenant Harris informed her that because she's twenty years old and considered an adult, the decision to tell her parents was hers to make."

"So now what?"

"In her role as dean of students, Babs will convene a judicial hearing, and the college's wheels of justice will begin to turn. I suppose for starters, Priscilla and Jen will be placed on probation, and maybe even the whole sorority house. I have no clue what the police will do. The only thing I know for certain is, when it comes to possession of fireworks, Ohio law is pretty strict."

Ruthalice leaned forward, took Cliff's head in both hands, and kissed his mouth.

"I've got it!" Cliff exclaimed through their pressed lips. "I finally remember the quote I couldn't come up with before."

Ruthalice rolled back onto her pillow. "Let's hear it," she said.

"What a tangled web we weave when first we practice to deceive."

"Ah, Sir Walter Scott." Ruthalice laid her left hand on Clifford's bare thigh. "He had such a way with words!"

## CHAPTER THIRTY-EIGHT

By three o'clock Thursday afternoon, Ruthalice had wrestled with her urge to "do something about Gideon" and pondered her options until her brain hurt. The bare branches still dripped, and dark gray clouds loomed on the horizon, but the cold morning rain had quit. The sun peeked weakly through the clouds, taunting her to come outside. Ruthalice snatched her red polka dot umbrella, hiked the six blocks to 534 Sheppard Place, and pounded on the kitchen door.

"Dummy," she scolded herself. "Charles is on campus. Gideon's not going to answer the door."

She punched three numbers in her cell phone before it dawned on her Gideon wouldn't answer the phone either. She propped the half-collapsed umbrella against the wall, jerked the door open, and stomped into Charles' cozy kitchen. *Gideon's going to have a heart attack whether I storm the fortress or tippy-toe in, so let's go for deafening.*

"Gideon, it's me, Ruthalice Michels." Her voice reverberated across the room. Hearing nothing but her own breathing, Ruthalice opened the basement door and hollered down the stairs.

Aware of movement behind her, Ruthalice turned around. Gideon materialized in front of the loveseat, his face barely visible in the dim light leaking through the threadbare curtains.

"I am here, Ruthalice, ma'am." Ruthalice strained to catch the words. "I am frightened when I hear someone knocking on the door. I hide behind the chair." He bowed from the waist, his face glowing. "Now you are my guest and are welcome in my new home. Please, you sit here," he added, pointing at the wingback chair. "I get us something to drink."

Gideon rummaged around in the refrigerator, looking for something to offer his unexpected guest. He reappeared in front of her chair and handed Ruthalice one of the professor's mismatched glasses. "Here," he said proudly, "I take the stripes; you are the flowers!"

They sipped the lemonade, comfortable with the gentle silence. Ruthalice surveyed the familiar living room with its jumble of bachelor paraphernalia accumulated over a lifetime of indifference to interior décor. Of the two wingback chairs, hers with its frayed armrests, was clearly the favorite. The best that could be said about the thin cotton drapes is they slowed down the light while providing a modicum of privacy. The meticulously polished wooden harpsichord was the exception to an indifference to craftsmanship. Safely tucked into the northeast corner of the living room, the little piano gave witness to the story that Charles Eugene Hopkins built this handcrafted beauty because the ones on offer were not up to snuff.

Ruthalice set her empty glass on the side table. "Are you happy here, Gideon?" She watched his eyes dart around the room. "I'm concerned about you always having to hide. That's why I am asking."

A look of resignation settled on his face. "I know how to hide," he said. "As a little boy I hide from my drunk uncle who comes to my mother when her husband is gone." He lifted his head and fixed Ruthalice with a dreadful stare. "I hear my mother crying 'No! No!' but I can do nothing." The skin tightened over his clenched jaw. "I hide after my mother and my little sister get killed at the house of my grandmother in the bombing of Baidoa."

Gideon walked across the room and sat in the empty wingback chair.

"There is too much fighting in my town of Doolow. When I go to school as a child, we hide from the fighters. The teachers say the soldiers will kill us. I hide after I get no more green card. Now I hide in basement of my friend, Professor Curly." He shrugged his narrow shoulders. "What does it matter where I hide?"

Torn between a longing to embrace this resilient young man and her penchant for offering practical suggestions, Ruthalice could neither move nor speak. All words of advice and comfort that came to mind sounded like tired platitudes. *What does God's love-in-action look like? Indeed, Amanda, how do we love our neighbor as ourselves?*

"There is no government in Somalia now," Gideon continued in that straightforward way of his. "There is no control over people in the north where my town is. Muslim terrorists pledge allegiance to Al Qaeda and plot to overthrow Somalia transitional government. The USA does not like Somalia. It is a safe place for terrorists, they say."

Ruthalice closed her eyes as the litany of violence grew. *You sound so matter-of-fact, dear Gideon, as though speaking your lines for a performance. Perhaps that is the only way you can speak about the atrocity that is present-day Somalia.*

"The United Nations tells the world Somalia is worst humanitarian crisis of any country in Africa. Al Shabaab say the World Food Program is anti-Islamic, so it stops aid from reaching the countryside. Over one million of my people are starving. Many more will die."

"But Gideon, if you stay in the States, you can't let your guard down for an instant. You will always be a fugitive, running and hiding from the law."

"If I go back to Somalia, I must watch my backside all the time. No," he insisted, shaking his head, "it is much better I stay in USA."

"You will never be able to have a normal life," she protested.

"What is normal life, Miss Ruthalice? In Somalia it is run, hide from soldiers, always run, always hide. But in America, soldiers don't kill me. They put me in detention, but they do not torture me." His voice tightened with resolve. "Until ICE deport me, I stay here, here with Professor Curly." His amazing smile returned without a trace of animosity. "Professor promise I stay with him and we figure out what to do next."

"I cannot bear the thought of you always on the lam, forced to disappear into some godforsaken hole in order to survive." She interlaced her fingers and raised them to her mouth. "My prayer for you, dear Gideon, is that you are free to stand in the sunshine, unafraid. Yes, above all else, unafraid."

"Where is this place, Miss Ruthalice," he asked wistfully, "where I stand in the sunshine, unafraid?" He reached across and lightly touched her arm. "Not here in Oakes Quarry, not in Mogadishu, not in USA, not in Somalia. Tell me where this place is, and I go there."

His gaze sought the photo of Charles' parents celebrating their tenth wedding anniversary. "I do not know what unafraid feel like except on my knees with Jesus."

Gideon walked over and squatted down beside the harpsichord, his eyes level with the professors' young parents. "Serita died in childbirth."

"Did you give the child a name before you buried her?" Ruthalice asked gently.

"Grace," he replied. "Grace Marie Boseka. Serita die in birth, but Grace live one week in incubator." He stood up and bowed his head. "They all leave me, my mother, my sister, my father, my wife and baby daughter—everybody leave me but Jesus."

"You have the faith that moves mountains, Gideon Boseka. I do not know anyone with such strength."

"You not know very many Somalis, Miss Ruthalice," he said kindly. "We learn to trust only God." He took a step forward. "I am sometimes very afraid, but not alone now. I have you and Clifford and Professor Curly." He placed his hand against his throat and lightly touched the cross with his fingertips. "I hope someday I am husband and father again."

Ruthalice felt as though a warm hand had just touched her heart. "You have much to teach me about suffering and endurance, my friend." She stood up, walked to the loveseat and picked up the battle-scarred Bible. Turning to Psalm 51 she began to read, "'Create in me a clean heart, oh God, and put a new and right spirit within me.'" She closed the Bible. "That is my prayer, Gideon. I came here this afternoon convinced I knew better than you did what you should do next, and I learned I know nothing. You are the expert here, Gideon, not Ruthalice Michels."

She placed the Bible on the smooth surface of the harpsichord. "Charles is a good man and a faithful friend. I'm sure he will do everything in his power to help you, Gideon, as will Cliff and I."

"You and Professor Clifford are my new best friends." His eyes lit up. "Maybe I come and work for you; make a big garden and grow many foods. Up on the hill in the woods no one know I am there," he added confidently. "People will say it is mystery that the garden of the M&Ms grow so tall and strong."

"The M&M Magnificent Magical Monster Garden. I love it." Ruthalice clasped her hands to her chest. "I must go now, Gideon. Is there anything you need I can get for you?"

"A new green card?" Gideon chuckled. "Yes, I think a new green card is nice."

"Don't I wish I could," she replied sincerely. "But until I can do that, how about dinner with us again this Sunday?"

"I come and cook flat bread and make chicken small-small. That is chicken stew with lots of vegetables," he explained, rubbing his stomach. "It is very yummy-good Somali dish."

"It's a date. Cliff and I will expect you and Charles and chicken small-small at one o'clock Sunday afternoon."

"I tell him call M&M," he laughed again as they walked to the kitchen door.

Gideon remained by the kitchen window watching her walk down the driveway. "I make grocery list for Professor Curly," he murmured happily. "Then we cook chicken small-small."

## CHAPTER THIRTY-NINE

S till musing happily about the Magical Monster Garden, Ruthalice started up the Frame Meeting-house steps when she spotted the police car in the campus minister's parking space, its motor running. Lieutenant Harris placed her officer's hat snuggly on top of her jet-black curls, climbed out of the squad car, and waited, clipboard in hand. Ruthalice noted the lieutenant's no-nonsense demeanor and felt her palms grow sticky. *There will be no 'Hi Ruthalice with an 'i' this time 'round.*

"I think I told you I stopped an African male in the warehouse parking lot a few days ago, and he led me to believe he's at Emerick College. Later you told me the only African student on campus is a man named Luther Mouana." Lieutenant Harris looked down at her black leather boots. "Now, I'm a little confused here." Her dark eyes hardened as she met the campus minister's resolute stare.

"That is correct. Luther is the only African student currently enrolled at EC."

"Well, I met Luther this afternoon," Rosemarie said, examining the fingernail polish on her right hand, "and he's a good six inches taller than the male I questioned. So, now I am asking you, Ms. Michels, who is this shorter African male?"

The lieutenant tapped her clipboard against her leg. "Perhaps I am being a bit unfair here by assuming you know everyone on campus." She brushed off a large

brown leaf that had landed on the shoulder of her navy-blue police jacket.

"What is this all about, Lieutenant?" Ruthalice
asked as calmly as possible. "I don't understand your
interest in him."

"Just curious, that's all." Her eyes softened. "The
arson investigation is officially complete, Ruthalice. I'm
just following up on a personal hunch that there's a
connection between the Penn Place fire and the man I
stopped in the Warehouse parking lot."

Ruthalice tried to unobtrusively release her held
breath and extended her hand to cover up her alarm.
"Rosemarie Harris," she said, wrapping her fingers
around the officer's warm hand, "I want you on my side
if I ever find myself in trouble with the law."

"Just being thorough," she said. She placed her
right hand on the door handle and turned to face Ruthalice. "Look, we both have a difficult job to do," Rosemarie began, "and I thought you'd appreciate hearing
the nature of my concern." The lieutenant shifted uncomfortably from one foot to the other. "And the fact
that duty required me to share my gut feeling with the
Chief." She tossed her cap on the front seat and gave
Ruthalice a self-conscious half-smile. "I want you to
know that professional courtesy and respect are at the
top of my list."

"Mine too," Ruthalice whispered as she watched
the black-and-white turn onto Division Street. "And
thanks for the cautionary tale, Lieutenant Rosemarie
Harris, sometimes known as Rosi with an 'i.'"

Just after supper, the Emerick College International
Student Club gathered around the wooden table in the

back corner of the Leaky Cup Café. Luther and Rani walked over together after supper, bundled up against the damp wind. Rani unwound the thick wool scarf Mary Scott gave her last year for Christmas. Resembling a large turtle, Luther hunkered down inside the hooded Emerick College sweatshirt his roommate's mother insisted he needed here in Ohio.

"Olga and Bodil are here," Rani announced happily as the two Swedes made their way to the table.

Olga pulled out a chair and began to unbutton her snowflake-covered ski sweater. Bodil extracted a notebook from her bookbag and waved at Rene, who sauntered across the cafe whistling under his breath. When they were all assembled around the table, Bodil dated the top of the page then slipped a loose strand of hair behind her ear.

"OK, let's get started planning the International Dinner and Dance."

Twenty minutes later, after everyone had been given an assignment, they fell into companionable chatter. Rani shot a quick glance at Luther and seeing the anxiety in his eyes, reached for his hand under the table.

"We have something important to share with you tonight." Startled by his serious tone of voice, the three friends stopped talking and stared at Luther. "Guys, this is all super confidential." Luther leaned into the circle. "I mean really, REALLY confidential."

Four heads nodded in understanding. "You can totally count on us, Luther," Bodil said. She clicked her ballpoint pen and set it on the notebook signaling the official end of minute taking.

"My cousin was hiding in the basement of Penington Place for the past few months." The students stared in astonishment. "When the fire started, he ran to Professor Hopkins' house for refuge."

Luther took a deep breath and brought both hands up from under the table. He laid them palms down on the surface in front of him.

"Now my cousin is in danger because his green card expired. If Immigration catches up with him, he will be deported back to Somalia."

Rani fingered the fringe on her red neck scarf. "I assured Luther that if our club knew about his cousin, we would help." Three heads nodded in agreement.

"My cousin is a coyote and a darn good one," Rene said. "He runs dozens of Mexicans safely across the border every year. I know he will take your cousin into Mexico really cheap."

"My God, Rene, what on earth are you talking about? We are not taking my cousin to Mexico, legally or illegally." Luther glared across the table. "Besides, what possible good would that do?"

"It would get him out of the country for one thing," Rene retorted, sliding back into this chair. "I'm just saying..."

"I think we should talk with Ruthalice Michels," Rani said.

"The campus minister?" Rene snorted. "What on earth for? I doubt she'll come up with anything we can't figure out all by ourselves." He shot an irritated look at Luther. "Didn't you just tell us to keep this information confidential?"

"Ruthalice already knows," Luther responded. "Professor Hopkins invited her and her husband to have dinner with me and Gideon Friday night." He smiled. "The campus minister already knows all about my cousin."

"I think Rani has a good idea," Olga said.

"Well, I can talk with Ruthalice tomorrow after Bible class." Bodil looked around the table. "Could you guys meet in her office at noon if she's free that is?" All heads nodded. "OK, I'll text you and we'll plan to be in her office tomorrow at noon."

Mollified now that a course of action had been agreed upon, Rene helped Olga carry their mugs to the communal sink. Luther took Rani's hand and led her back across campus. When they reached Penington Place, he led her around to the back.

"That is how my cousin got in and out," he said, pointing at the coal bin door barely visible behind the bushes. He lowered his head and began to trace a circle in the grass with his left foot.

"What's wrong, Luther?"

"I don't know if we did the right thing tonight, Rani." He stuffed both hands into the front pocket of his hoodie. "I just hope Rene keeps his mouth shut."

"Me too," she agreed softly. "Me too."

# CHAPTER FORTY

Bodil waited until the circle of students surrounding Ruthalice had dispersed.

"Can I talk to you a minute?"

"Of course, Bodil."

"The International Club wonders if we can meet with you today at noon."

"Let's go check my calendar." The two women walked into her office. "Looks good. May I ask what this is about?"

"Something came up last night at our club meeting. We agreed it would be better to talk with you before doing anything about the situation."

"OK then, see all of you at noon."

Ruthalice spent the next hour laying preliminary plans for the third annual A Day of Thanksgiving Festival to be held the first week in November. As promised, the five international students were taking their seats around her coffee table by the time the carillon finished striking twelve.

"So, what's on your minds?" Ruthalice asked, as they unwrapped scarves and shrugged out of various jackets. Four sets of eyes stared at Luther, appointing him as their spokesperson.

"I, Rani and I," Luther paused and glanced at Rani's face making sure it was still all right to include her. At her nod he continued, "Last night, Rani and I told the International Club about Gideon."

A look of alarm sped across Ruthalice's face.

"The International Club wants to help Gideon get legal status in the United States," Rani explained.

Despite the apprehension gripping every cell in her body, Ruthalice's heart went out to these eager young people. "I wish that were possible," she said smiling sadly. "And I know I'm going to sound like a wet blanket here, but persuading the INS to make an exception in Gideon's case is simply not going to happen."

"Why not?" Rene shot back. He didn't try to hide his "I-told-you-so" glare at the other students.

"Well, for starters," Ruthalice began, ignoring Rene's glare, "there is no wiggle room in the Immigration and Naturalization Service rules. Since 1996 US law states anyone who has been in this country illegally for more than one year is barred from immigrating to the United States until they have first returned to their home country and lived there for ten years."

"Ten years!" Olga wailed. "The whole world knows how dangerous Somalia is. Gideon could get killed. That's just plain not fair."

"Unfortunately, it doesn't matter what we think, Bodil. Fair or not, it's the way things are these days, and pretending otherwise is counterproductive at best. Believe me, Olga," Ruthalice said grimly, "I hate this as much as you do."

Ruthalice leaned back and surveyed the little circle. "You can't challenge Gideon's status without calling attention to his presence in our community, and the minute you do that, ICE will swoop in and detain him. They are removing undocumented Somali refugees in unprecedented numbers. I don't know how to be any plainer than that."

"So are we just going to ignore this injustice and sit around doing nothing?" Spittle and words tumbled out of Rene's mouth in an angry spray.

"I did not say that, Rene. What I am saying is we've got to be very cautious and weigh all the consequences. We cannot be the ones to decide Gideon's future for him." Ruthalice leaned forward in her chair. "I will tell you one thing in confidence," she began, looking at each student in turn around the circle, "Gideon trusts Professor Hopkins with his life. He told me on Thursday that he and the professor will figure out what to do next."

"If any of us messes this up," Luther said, "and my cousin ends up in shackles on a plane bound for Mogadishu because somebody reports him—"

A grim silence settled on the room as the students stared at the floor, avoiding eye contact.

"We must not share this idea with any of our friends," Rani said, "because the more people who find out Gideon is here, the less safe he is."

"It sounds as though we are all clear that mum's the word," Ruthalice said, getting to her feet. "Let me make a few phone calls, and I will call us together again when and if there are some options that make sense. In the meantime, just keep reminding yourselves that Gideon is safe for the time being with Charles Hopkins. We don't want to do anything to jeopardize that situation."

The students rose as one and began collecting backpacks, scarves, and gloves.

"By the way," Ruthalice said, "let me tell you what Ann Richards, the former governor of Texas said. 'Life isn't fair. I know life isn't fair, but government should be.'"

She waited by her office door until the students left the building, then sank heavily into the nearest chair.

She buried her face in her hands and slowed her breathing until her fear subsided and her mind became clear. Then, lifting her wool cape off the clothes tree, she headed to Fox Hall.

"It's open." Charles looked up from his reading as she knocked on his door jam. "And to what do I owe this honor?"

"I've come to tell you about a meeting I just had with the International Club students."

When she had finished, Charles lay his red pen down on the papers in front of him, removed his reading glasses, and stared at Ruthalice with bloodshot eyes.

"Charles, all five of them know about Gideon," Ruthalice said, her stomach clenching as his jaw tightened. "The club believes to a person that if they sponsor him and convince the INS it's too dangerous for him to return to Somalia, he will be allowed to remain in the US."

Something flickered in the back of the old professor's eyes.

"Not possible."

"I managed to hold them off temporarily by urging them not to do anything that puts Gideon's safety at risk. They pledged themselves to secrecy, but I honestly don't know how long that will last."

Charles placed his fists on the desk and rose to his feet.

"Idealism has its limits, Ruthalice, and good intentions get you only so far." He leaned forward. "Remember, my dear, the road to hell is full of them."

"Charles, there is something I must ask you to think about. Is there any good reason to contact Immigration?"

"Good God, no!" he thundered. "A man's life is at stake here, Ruthalice. This is hardly the time for wishful thinking." He came around the desk. "Thank you for stopping by, Ruthalice," he said shrugging into his overcoat.

"I'm just like those students," she said longingly. "We all want a happy ending."

"The world is too messy for neat and tidy endings, my dear Ruthalice." He patted her on the shoulder, stepped into the hallway, and hurried down the corridor.

Ruthalice remained in the doorway. "I was hoping you would provide all the answers, Charles," she said softly. *No, I wanted a miracle worker.* "Maybe so," she said aloud and smiled, "but my goodness, how dear Charles would scoff at the very idea."

## CHAPTER FORTY-ONE

His mind made up, Charles Hopkins scurried across the parking lot and started the cantankerous little VW. As he pulled out of the lot, he narrowly missed turning into a red pickup truck barreling down the street. The driver hit the horn, swerved, and gave him the finger.

"First stop is Wal-Mart for a suitcase," Charles muttered to himself. "The lad also needs a winter coat, gloves, wool cap, and he can't keep wearing those same two shirts."

The shopping completed, he tossed two large shopping bags and a plaid, soft-sided suitcase on the back seat. He swung by the local car rental agency, drove back through town to Sheppard Place, and walked into the living room.

"Gideon," he said, addressing his young guest seated in the accustomed spot on the loveseat, "we've been cooped up in this house long enough. We're taking a road trip this weekend." He dropped the plastic bags on the rug beside his feet.

"I called our friend Terrell Martin. We are going up to Toledo for a visit. And to be sure we arrive there safely, I have rented a car for the occasion."

Gideon grinned. "A trip adventure, Professor Curly." His face suddenly clouded. "But I tell the M&Ms we come for dinner on Sunday. I promise to cook."

Charles replied airily, "Oh, that's all right. I informed Ruthalice this afternoon that we would be out of town this weekend. She said to come out some other time." He pointed to the suitcase by the basement door. "Gideon, there's a new suitcase for you. A few new shirts, a sweater, and winter outer garments are in these plastic bags."

"My goodness, Professor Curly, I take all that to Toledo?"

"It's much colder that far north," Charles insisted firmly. "Now, go and pack all your things, including your Bible and anything else you brought to my house." Gideon looked puzzled. "Martin wants you to stay with him for a few weeks until I can free up another weekend at the college and get back up to collect you."

Gideon nodded and did as instructed. Twenty minutes later he was back in the kitchen, his new coat draped over his right arm. "I ready to go to Toledo." He indicated the small brown valise resting by the back door. "You are taking not much, Professor Curly."

"A fellow my age travels light. Oh, by the way, do you happen to have your uncle's phone number in Minnesota? I thought it would be jolly good fun to give him a ring whilst we're in Toledo."

"Call my cousin? I not talk with my cousin for months!" Digging in his pocket, Gideon extracted a small notebook. "I have it here," he said turning the worn pages. "Yes, it is here, Professor Curly."

"Now be a good lad and double check your room to be sure you have everything. I'll meet you in the car. The agent delivered it while you were in the basement packing."

Charles took the new Gore-Tex jacket from where Gideon had laid it on the counter and slipped two one-hundred-dollar bills into the inner pocket. He ran his fingers along the Velcro strip, sealing them safely inside, and laid the jacket back down for Gideon to pick up on his way outside. He put the suitcases in the trunk of the rental car and climbed into the driver's seat. Drumming his fingers on the steering wheel, he waited impatiently until Gideon slipped in beside him and buckled his seat belt.

"We take an adventure trip in a fine new car." Gideon beamed at the professor. "When I come to Emerick College, Dr. Martin live in Oakes Quarry." He shook his head. "That was a very long time ago."

"A lot of water's gone under the bridge since then, hasn't it, my young friend?" Charles backed out of the driveway, turned on the headlights, and headed north out of town. "It's a long trip, Gideon," he warned. "Why don't you try to sleep a little?"

"No, no," he laughed lightly. "I want to watch. I like to see all the lights. In Somalia it is very dark at night." He stared intently out the window. "I stay awake and keep you company, Professor Curly, then we sleep at Dr. Martin's house." Gideon continued to gaze into the night. "I like lights, Professor Curly," he added solemnly. "Then I see what is going to happen next."

# CHAPTER FORTY-TWO

"**M**y gosh, eight-thirty already." Cliff located his slippers with his right heel and padded into the living room. He bent over and kissed the top of Ruthalice's head. "How long you been up?"

"Since about five. I gave up after a persistent case of the four-o'clock-wobblies." She closed the Bible and patted the space beside her on the green leather couch. "Come sit."

"So, what's got you all stirred up?" Cliff refilled her mug from the thermos on the coffee table and smiled. Ruthalice's glasses fogged up as she inhaled the steamy coffee smell.

"Is this fire someone's fault or just bad luck?" She frowned. "What's that saying about the whole and its parts? The whole can't exist if one of its parts is missing, or something like that." She brought her right leg up and tucked her heel under her left knee to hold everything in place. "It seems to me that the irony is each one of these people—Priscilla, Jen, Ira, Richard and his decision to store overstuffed furniture under the stairs—is individually both innocent and guilty."

"It's all about hiding," Cliff said. Ruthalice gave him a startled look. "The most obvious being Gideon in the coal bin; the nefarious loot in the cubbyhole being another."

"And secrets," Ruthalice said. "Ira kept his smoking a secret and as always happens with secrets, your primary concern quickly becomes making sure nobody finds out what you are up to."

"And the consequences be damned."

Ruthalice carried her mug to the plate glass window and drew open the heavy drapes. A pair of wild turkeys strutted across the backyard, pausing here and there to peck at something that caught their attention in the grass.

"I want to back up to what I said earlier about the whole and the missing parts."

"OK, let's hear it."

"I'm thinking of this as an equation that goes like this: fireworks, plus a burning cigarette, plus overstuffed chairs, equals conflagration. If you remove any of the variables on the left-hand side, we get a different result."

"If I may do a bit of math-speak here," Cliff offered, watching his wife's face. Ruthalice grinned and nodded her permission. "Solving the equation consists of determining which values of the variables make the equation true. Sometimes variables are also unknowns. So we can ask the question, Which values make the equation true?"

Ruthalice placed her palm against the windowpane. "Fireworks plus lighted cigarette butt plus stored furniture equals fire plus the human tragedy of disrupted lives." She lifted her hand and watched her print evaporate.

"In Curly's case, the predictability of his bachelor existence has been seriously derailed. I am certain necessity has placed Bishop Swithun, albeit reluctantly, on the back burner."

"And Richard who has devoted hours to the investigation, attended countless meetings, issued press releases..." her voice trailed off.

Cliff joined her at the window, placed both hands on her shoulders, and turned her around.

"And let us not forget the campus minister, Sweetheart. That woman is running herself ragged and hasn't had a decent night's sleep in over a week." He kissed her forehead, then pulled her tight against him.

Ruthalice wrapped her arms around his waist and pressed her cheek against his chest.

"I can't stop worrying about Gideon." She leaned back in order to see Cliff's face. "He told me he can't even begin to imagine what truly safe would feel or look like." She took Cliff's hand and interlocked their fingers. "You know, Cliff, when I marched over to Curly's house on Thursday, I was dead certain the best solution for Gideon was to get this over with, turn himself in, and head back to Somalia. When I left an hour later, I was equally certain Gideon would be committing suicide if he followed my advice."

"I've started thinking of him as Gideon the Innocent," Cliff said softly. He smoothed the soft hair on top of Ruthalice's head and looked into her eyes. "Have you given further thought about what to do now that the international students have gotten into the act?"

"Not really. I can't even decide whether to write my congressman and rail against inhumane regulations or go find a corner and bawl my head off, let alone figure out how to head off our well-meaning students."

"What about giving Terrell Martin a call? He's got a vested interest in Gideon. He might have some contacts after his work with the UN in Mogadishu, so there's a good chance he knows somebody at INS. He might even have a suggestion or two."

"Maybe so." She smiled up at him. "But for right now I'm going to heed my own advice and not rush into anything. If contacting Martin feels like the way forward, I'll give him a call."

"Well in that case, I have another idea." Cliff took her hands in his. "It is so nice outside, how about we go to the men's soccer match this afternoon. We can hit Damon's for supper after the game."

"This Friend speaks my mind," she said grinning, "and thus requires no further thinking on my part."

# CHAPTER FORTY-THREE

The M&Ms walked along the chain-link fence and joined the cluster of faithful faculty and enthusiastic students seated on gray metal bleachers at midfield. The PA system gave a squawk, then settled down to a low-level hum.

"Ladies and gentlemen. Please rise for the singing of our national anthem."

"And the home of the brave," Ruthalice sang. "That voice sounds very familiar, Cliff." She leaned against his shoulder. "Do you know who the announcer is?" Cliff shook his head and sat back down. Ruthalice twisted around and stared up into the glass-enclosed press box ten rows behind them.

"I knew that voice sounded familiar, Cliff. It's Ted Cope. Look," she said, resisting the urge to point. "Stevens must have made him team statistician and PA announcer for today's game."

As the Mighty Quakers trotted off the field with a ninth win in their pockets, Cliff gave Ruthalice a nudge. "Look," he said nodding toward a heavily bundled-up fan two rows down. "It's Sidney Cope." Ted's uncle got to his feet, raised his arms, and gave a two-handed thumbs-up toward the press box. His nephew returned both the gesture and the grin.

"The unpredictable Sidney Cope," Ruthalice said. "Will wonders never cease?"

Cliff placed both hands on her shoulders as they slowly worked their way along the bleacher rows and down to field level. "What do you say we go eat?"

Cliff snagged a discarded *Oakes Quarry Gazette* from the hostess desk as the waitress led them to their table. While they waited for their order to arrive, he turned to the sports section leaving the rest of the paper for Ruthalice. He was halfway through an article on the undefeated Oakes Quarry High School football team led by senior Russell Harris, when Ruthalice gripped his arm.

"What is it, Ruthalice?" She tapped the newspaper with her index finger. "You'd better read it to me, Sweetheart."

"The FBI has contacted the Oakes Quarry police department with information concerning the hiring practices of Smart Outlet Warehouses, Inc. Due to the large number of illegal aliens employed by the chain nationwide (some estimates as high as 750 individuals), all locations have come under surveillance. The Oakes Quarry store located on McKaig Avenue issued a statement late Friday afternoon indicating they do not employ undocumented workers. An outside investigation of regional employee records has begun."

Cliff dropped a few dollars on the table beside their untouched water glasses and, without a word, the M&Ms drove straight to Sheppard Place. Ruthalice pounded on the kitchen door, while Clifford jabbed the front doorbell.

"Listen, Charles Hopkins, we're getting really worried here." Ruthalice muttered after all their noise was met with a profound silence. She scribbled 'Call the M&Ms ASAP' on her soccer program and slipped it under the back door, then walked around the building. She surveyed the postage-stamp-sized backyard. A half-empty finch feeder dangled from a hook screwed into the gum tree a few yards from the house.

"Maybe they went to Cincinnati for the day," Cliff offered, but knew, even as he said it, the probability that the little VW was up to the trip was minimal at best.

Ruthalice walked to the garage and peered through the dirty pane of glass. "His car's still here," she announced, looking back at Cliff. She headed back to the house, jiggled the knob, and shoved. The kitchen door swung open without a hitch. The M&Ms exchanged a conspiratorial smile and stepped into Professor Charles Hopkins' wheat-and-yellow kitchen.

The house was filled with the no-sound of an empty space. Cliff flipped the light switch and trotted down the basement steps. Rumpled bedding was the only indication someone had slept there. He did a quick survey of the room then pulled the sheets and blanket off the cot and placed them on top of the washing machine. After checking under the bed, Cliff slowly climbed the stairs.

"They're gone," Ruthalice said.

"It would appear so. There's not a single item belonging to Gideon in the basement."

"I looked in the back bedroom. Charles's bed is made, which makes me wonder if they slept somewhere else last night." She sighed. "I don't have a good feeling about any of this right now."

"I'd say the fact the VW is still in the garage indicates something longer than a day trip."

Ruthalice pulled out her iPhone, tapped the map search app, and dialed the number on her screen.

"This is Ruthalice Michels, campus minister at Emerick College. Can you tell me whether Professor Charles Hopkins rented a car from you yesterday?" She traced a circle on the smooth mahogany surface of the harpsichord while she waited. "Thank you."

"I gather from the look on your face that was a 'yes.'"

"A Charles Hopkins came in it at two-thirty and rented a Focus for the weekend. It's due back by nine o'clock Monday morning." Ruthalice looked down at her feet and sighed. "I think they're in trouble, Cliff. What if Immigration has caught wind of Gideon?"

"If the authorities have already gone through the warehouse hiring records, I suppose anything's possible. However, I wouldn't advise trying to catch up with Gideon's boss lady, Ruthalice," Cliff said, touching her cheek with his fingers. "You might stir up more questions than answers."

"I know," she said, kissing the palm of his hand. "Anything we do now that involves officialdom runs the risk of blowing this whole refugee thing wide open."

"Hiding and secrets," Cliff reminded her softly, "the modus operandi for this entire affair."

"Do you think Charles has panicked?" Cliff frowned. "With the FBI and INS snooping around, I mean."

"Charles Hopkins will not panic even if he knows about the investigation of the local Warehouse Store. A man of his experience and stature views panic as weakness."

Cliff turned off the overhead and reached for Ruthalice's hand.

"Come on, Sweetheart, there's nothing more we can do here." He led the way through the kitchen and out the back door. "By the way, weren't Charles and Gideon planning on coming to Horsefeathers Farm tomorrow for Sunday dinner?"

"That's right. Gideon is cooking chicken small-small. In fact, he insisted on buying all the ingredients himself," she added cheerfully.

"Then let's just go home and sit tight and see what tomorrow brings."

## CHAPTER FORTY-FOUR

"Good heavens we're popular today," Ruthalice muttered, picking up her cell phone after the second round of "It's a Small World After All." As she listened, she watched the curved tail swing effortlessly back and forth on the black-cat wall clock, its white ping-pong-ball eyes surveying the kitchen with their sightless gaze. The garish red-arrow hands stood at right angles at one fifteen on the cat's round tummy.

Ruthalice slipped the cell phone into the pocket of her skirt and joined Cliff in the bedroom.

"Barbara Carroll just called to let me know the college judicial review board met earlier this morning and placed both Priscilla Brinkley and Jennifer Blake on probation for the rest of the academic year. Another infraction and they are suspended from Emerick College. They also are required to give written apologies to the board of trustees, as well as the fire and police departments."

"Ah, the old kitchen sink treatment." Cliff hung his suit coat on a hanger and reached for the L.L. Bean flannel shirt on the back of the ladderback chair. "Did she say anything about repercussions related to the State of Ohio statutes on fireworks?"

"All she said was the authorities are taking the necessary steps required under state law."

"That's got an ominous ring to it."

"I doubt anyone's amused by this enormously expensive little caper." Ruthalice changed out of her Sunday-go-to-meeting clothes into her favorite knee-length tunic and black leggings. "Be a dear, would you, and lay another fire. We can wait to light it until Charles and Gideon get here." She followed Cliff into the living room. Pale streaks of sunlight worked their way through heavy gray clouds filling the sky. Even with the curtains drawn back, the room was dark. "On second thought, Sweetheart, light it now. It's chilly and depressing in here."

Ruthalice raised her arm and squinted at her watch. "Something just doesn't feel right. They were supposed to be here at two, so Gideon could start cooking." She opened and closed her fists in a vain attempt to release the tension in her arms. "OK, I'm going to sit down right here," she said dropping onto the green sofa, "and stew until Gideon and Charles appear on our doorstep."

By half-past four, Ruthalice could sit still no longer. She wandered into the kitchen and stopped at the end of the breakfast nook where Cliff sat grading lab notebooks. "I've called the house every half-hour since two-thirty this afternoon," she said. "And I just got off the phone with Luther, who called to tell me that he and Rani are standing in the professor's driveway wondering what to do next."

"They went to Charles' house?" Cliff leaned back and frowned. "Whatever for?"

"They're afraid one of the international club students may have spoken out of turn, and they wanted to talk with Professor Hopkins."

"Or maybe they've heard about the employee records investigation at the Warehouse and think Gideon is on the government's radar screen."

"OK, that does it, Cliff. I'm going in." Ruthalice extracted the car keys from her canvas bag and slung the strap over her shoulder. "And, no," she said, opening the mudroom door, "I don't need any help." She blew him an air kiss. "But I promise to be in touch after I figure out what's actually going on."

To her enormous relief, a white Ford Focus sat in the driveway of 534 Sheppard Place when she arrived. A gold bumper sticker with white lettering announced: "This vehicle could be your ride—Sure Rental Cars—Oakes Quarry, Ohio." Ruthalice marched to the side door and unceremoniously turned the knob, called out Charles's name, and walked in. She sidestepped the little brown valise sitting exactly where Charles had dropped it an hour earlier when sheer exhaustion threatened to topple him. His London Fog overcoat lay similarly discarded across the back of the first kitchen chair he came to inside the back door. She walked into the living room and spotted the well-scuffed brogues lying beside the loveseat. Their owner slouched in his favorite wingback chair with the threadbare armrest covers and comfortable low spot in the seat cushion.

"I'm frightfully sorry." Charles took a deep breath and tried again, "I apologize for missing dinner this afternoon, Ruthalice. I hope you and Clifford will forgive my ill manners in failing to call to explain our absence." He gave her a weak smile and held up his left hand. "You're sure you won't have a drop of brandy to fortify your constitution?"

Ruthalice declined with a shake of her head. Having fulfilled his welcoming responsibilities, Charles poured himself an ample shot, pressed his right temple against the wing of his chair and stared across the room, as Ruthalice settled into the corner of the loveseat. She crossed her arms and laid them on top of the sofa pillow she pulled into her lap.

"I know you are exhausted, Charles, so may I tell you what I think has happened here?" Ruthalice caught the minuscule nod and plunged ahead. "After our conversation on Friday, you decided Oakes Quarry was no longer a safe haven for Gideon. I'm guessing you called Terrell Martin for advice." She watched the professor's face to gauge whether she was getting the story straight. "Then what?"

"The lies began." Charles leaned to his left and pulled a rumpled handkerchief from his pants pocket. "Martin and I agreed the safest and most compassionate course of action was to deliver the boy to his extended family."

"You drove all the way to the Twin Cities?" Ruthalice covered her gasp with the back of her hand. He nodded. "And the lies?"

"I told Gideon we were going to Toledo for an extended stay. I was keeping the Twin Cities my little surprise for as long as I could manage it." His smile held a hint of self-satisfaction. "When the lad woke up early Saturday morning, he wanted to know if we were in Toledo yet. No, my young friend, I said, we are in the Twin Cities. I have brought you to your cousin's house." Charles spread open the rumpled-up handkerchief and blew his nose. "You should have seen Gideon's face, Ruthalice. I don't know which was more rewarding, the look of shock or the following look of sheer delight." Charles wiped his eyes with the dry tail of the handkerchief. "Gideon started to bawl like a baby."

Ruthalice swiped at the tears running silently down her cheeks and pooling on the end of her chin. She leaned over and used the hem of her skirt to dry her face.

"I wish you could have been there, Ruthalice." Charles rolled his head from side to side against the back of the armchair. "The entire front porch of this dilapidated frame house was overflowing with Somali refugees. I have never seen such a ragtag bunch of people so overcome with joy." Charles closed his eyes and smiled remembering how the gray-haired patriarch had warmly embraced him, heralding him as the guardian who delivered their long-lost relative back into the bosom of his extended family.

Charles raised his head and gazed at the photograph of his parents in its pride-of-place on the handmade harpsichord in the corner of the room.

"I realized this evening that in a lifetime of consequential decision making, this was my finest hour." A blush began to creep from his throat into his cheeks. "I was homeless, and you gave me shelter; I was naked, and you gave me a shirt; I was hungry, and you shared your porridge." He paused. "Am I close, Ruthalice?" he asked, smiling across at her. "You're the biblically-astute person in the room."

"You left out, I was in prison and you visited me there." She dropped the hem of her skirt back across her knees and felt the fabric fall to her ankles. "I want to add another one," she said, returning his smile. "I was smoked out of hiding into the precarious open, and you gave me refuge."

Neither spoke for a minute, allowing the ensuing silence to settle comfortably around them. Suddenly Charles leapt to his feet. Propelled by an unanticipated wave of loneliness, he charged down the basement stairs. Ruthalice found him sitting on the empty cot, his arms hanging limply between his legs. She stood in front of him and placed both hands on his shoulders.

"What a slobbery old fool I've turned into. All these decades I have jealously guarded my solitude, and now," he swept his right arm around the room, "I feel abandoned." The old professor laid his hands on top of Ruthalice's. "Was it truly only twelve days ago Gideon took flight and landed on my doorstep?"

"We get stretched sometimes to the breaking point, yet somehow manage to come out the other side with more compassion and love than we thought possible." Ruthalice took his hands and stepped back. "You know what I think, Professor Charles E. Hopkins? I think you and Gideon were the victims of the carelessness of others and because you both are experienced survivors you—" She swallowed and dropped his hands. "Well, let me just say, you came through with flying colors one more time."

"Thank you, Ruthalice," he said. "May I have the final word?" he asked, getting slowly to his feet.

"Of course," she replied.

"'For so the game is ended that should not have begun.'" Charles bowed gently from the waist. "Thank you, A. E. Housman," he said softly. "I could not have phrased it better myself."

www.ingramcontent.com/pod-product-compliance
Lightning Source LLC
Chambersburg PA
CBHW050504260626
47157CB00004B/1187